IN&OZ

also by Steve Tomasula

VAS: An Opera in Flatland

IN&OZ

a novel
by

Steve Tomasula

Ministry of Whimsy
Madison, Wisconsin/Tallahassee, Florida

Ministry of Whimsy Press
www.ministryofwhimsy.com

Ministry Editorial Offices:
Forrest Aguirre (editor)
1718 Weber Drive
Madison, WI 53713

ministryofwhimsy@yahoo.com

Ministry of Whimsy Press is an imprint of:
Night Shade Books:
3623 SW Baird Street
Portland, OR 97219

Design by: Crispin Prebys and Slip Studios

ABOUT THE MINISTRY OF WHIMSY
Founded in 1984 by Jeff VanderMeer, the Ministry of Whimsy takes its name from
the ironic double-speak of Orwell's novel. The Ministry is committed to promoting
high quality fantastical, surreal, and experimental literature. In 1997, the Ministry
published the Philip K. Dick Award-winning *The Troika*. In more recent years, its
flagship anthology series, *Leviathan*, has been a finalist for the Philip K. Dick Award
and the British Fantasy Award. Authors published by the Ministry, in books or
anthologies, include Rikki Ducornet, Michael Moorcock, Zoran Zivkovic, Lance
Olsen, Carol Emshwiller, and Brian Evenson.

ISBN: 1-892389-63-0

PRAISE FOR PREVIOUS FICTION

"...this novel constitutes a leap forward for the genre we call 'novel.' Collapsing nonfiction into fiction, women's reproductive concerns into men's, history into present, work into play — this novel takes juxtaposition and digression to new heights."
>   —Kass Fleisher, *American Book Review*

"...Steve Tomasula's baroque tour de force 'Bodies in Flatland.'"
>   —Rod Smith, *Rain Taxi*

A breathtaking inquiry into the artifacts of the human imagination, *VAS: An Opera in Flatland* is sensuous, ferocious, and original.
>   —Rikki Ducornet, *The Novelist*

Steve Tomasula's extraordinary "novel" —or is it a film script? collage art work? philosophical meditation? —tracks the story of a "simple" event in the life of a 21st century family. But "story" is the wrong word here, for Tomasula's dissection of post-biological life is about the new interaction of bodies and DNA possibilities. Tomasula's imagination, his satiric edge, his wildly comic sense of things, combined with inventive page lay-out make reading this "Opera in Flatland" an unforgettable experience.
>   —Marjorie Perloff, *The Critic*

VAS is an encyclopedic quest for three-dimensional thinking in a two-dimensional quadvaverse of cloned geneticists replicating racialist double binds. With striking visual aplomb, *VAS* casts factoids off the steps of the Temples of the Predetermined into the yet-to-be-written name of errant possibility.
>   —Charles Bernstein, *The Poet*

for Maria

IN&OZ

CHAPTER ONE

The dogs of IN are snarling again, snapping at each other and breaking their teeth against the bars of their pen.

They are mean dogs, dirty and of indeterminate breed but with the color and size of dogs associated with fascism. Their owner, similar in look and temperament, hates dogs. He only keeps them because he also keeps thousands of shiny tools that he needs for his one real passion, working on junk cars, in the garage behind his house, beside the pen he has made of welded rebar where the dogs spend their days fighting and barking and fucking and shitting and running back and forth, irritating themselves and each other until night falls and Mechanic puts them in the garage to protect the tools.

CHAPTER TWO

There are no dogs in OZ. Or rather, there are no real dogs. There are police dogs. And sheep dogs. And drug-sniffing dogs and watch dogs. But there are no car-chasing dogs. No garbage-can-upsetting dogs. No, need it be said, poet dogs. The streets are very clean and traffic moves at the speed of commerce, which is to say, as fast and smooth as a concept car on a victory lap as one woman, a Designer, might have put it, had she been at her drawing board instead of shopping.

Lap dog in hand, she entered one of the bookstores of OZ and immediately felt herself become more serious, informed by tradition, by quality. Being a designer, she was not oblivious to the role that the store itself played in this sense of herself that could be read in the body language of everyone browsing the aisles. Like them, she felt her motions slow to the dignified pace of a curator, or librarian, influenced as they were by the leisurely pace of music that played on a loop—beautiful, egg-head music that she would never listen to at home but enjoyed here because it had been mastered somehow to include only the bright tones and none of the darker, pathetic notes usually associated with music of that sort. Greek columns ran up the walls to where portraits of authors looked down from spots that were too high to hold product: portraits of difficult, aesthetic high-wire walkers from the last century as well as contemporary authors of cookbooks, based-on-fact thrillers, and other works that could actually be found in the store—all drawn in the style of engraving associated with the dead presidents on monetary notes so that even non-readers could understand their value.

Designer found it all particularly moving today since this was the day that the book featuring some of her own work was to appear in stores: a glossy, coffee-table art book documenting a recent showing of Automobiles that had been mounted at the Museum of OZ Art, and that was to have her best-selling sports coupe on the cover.

Approaching the books, she put down her dog so she would have both hands free and took her place among the other shoppers. Book after glossy book devoted to the beauty of Auto flowed by, their cover photos so slick that they seemed to be works of art in their own right—portraits of stretch limos with tricked-out doors, spray painted in lollipop greens and purples, car hoods that were Sistine chapels of air-brushed saints and angles, baby-blue clouds of acrylic heavenly hosts—a stream of books and magazines so hypnotically beautiful that they made it nearly impossible to select just one.

Indeed, in OZ, they had so refined the art of giving the customer what he or she wants that there are no books available that are not wanted by everyone. To Designer, like most of those too young to remember another way, this was just how it was—a state of nature. And in fact, it was the result of a sort of evolution: in the early days, a book would be displayed on a shelf only so long as it sold at a certain popular level. But as the speed of commerce increased, and the business of books (plural) decreased the time any one book (singular) might remain on a shelf, the bookshelves themselves began to lengthen, then move, evolving into extremely long conveyer belts that carried books directly from printing presses through the stores where customers were to this day compelled to quickly make their selection the way they might select sushi from a passing boat in a Japanese restaurant. That is, as with raw fish, freshness became the dominant concern. So instead of re-circulating back through the kitchen then out past the customers again, "printed matter" that no one plucked from the stream on a single pass continued on its one-way journey through the stores and into the recycling plants of IN. There it was shredded, and turned into products that people might find more useful, such as humorous calendars, greeting cards or the paper cups used in the coffee shops that took up most of the actual square footage of each bookstore. Since movies, cars, bottled water, perfume, art and all forms of entertainment were sold in exactly this way, culture had become like time in OZ—always the same, though no customer could ever dip his or her toe into the same stream twice. And without anyone even noticing, dogs, real dogs, somehow vanished.

In OZ, revolving doors are thought of with the nostalgia usually reserved for train stations.

CHAPTER THREE

The Mechanic's dogs are half mad, starved for attention as they are, crazed from hunger in order to "give them that edge." They go berserk whenever they catch sight of him, which is hundreds of times a day as he goes back and forth between his cinder-block house and his cinder-block garage.

Not long ago, Mechanic had been deaf to all of this. Though he passed them so often he had worn a rut in the yard between the house and the garage, he never so much as glanced at the dogs and their terrific noise. While neighbors of a man like this might be expected to be incensed at his neglect, by the racket of two huge dogs fighting in a pen all day, this man's neighbors are not. Before he got the dogs, they know, his garage was broken into. And tools stolen. So they accept the wet stench of dirty dogs and their shit, and the racket, and the fact that the yard looks brown and dead as if it were winter the year round— they dismiss these and many other "intangibles" for the greater good of the tools.

That is, they, as do all good citizens of IN, understand.

In IN, the Tractor-Trailer is King, and the Mobile Home Queen.

CHAPTER FOUR

Just as soldiers or nudists are able to identify each other by their dress, so a wordless language developed in OZ that allowed even the thinnest of demographic slivers to find mates, identify enemies, and do all the things people must do in order for their work-a-day lives to unfold. Many and diverse mouths contributed to the development of this language but the dominant voice issued from its clearest example: The Essence of OZ Building in which Designer worked, and which was in fact so tall that its shadow fell 'round the world. From a distance, this building had the aspect of a castle in the sky, its granite skin glittering in the sun. From her studio at its top, the world appeared Lilliputian below, a body of lesser skyscrapers and roads and bridges, including a rusty hump of a girder bridge that rose high above the flatland in the distance where it sutured OZ to IN.

Designer liked to take the art book whose cover sported one of her cars and stand it up on the windowsill, then contemplate the disjunction in scale created by the juxtaposition: the car on the cover, the simulacrum of a car, looked large, up close as it was, while outside the window, the real cars down below appeared tiny, and somehow this relationship seemed to hold more truth than it would if she were to take the photo of the car down to the street and let the real cars run over it.

Though she had won many awards for her designs of auto bodies, secretly, she never thought of herself as a designer of autos at all. True enough, her curvaceous fenders and hoods did mask the grotesque viscera of cars. But they did so in the way that an arty dress or designer eye-glasses were more of a language than an article of clothing or medical aide—a dominant language, the way French had once been the tongue of diplomacy, or Latin of conquest. If she wasn't giving desire form—and shaping the world by doing so— what exactly was she or any designer doing? Isn't this why women's blue jeans came in so many versions: The Flare (Slung Way, Way Low); The Boyfriend (The Relaxed Comfort of His Jeans); The Curve (Show Off YourS); The Capri (Gypsy Styling); The London Jean (High, High Inseam); The Carpenter (Baggy with Hammer Loops); The Hip-Hop (Trés Gangsta); The Natural (Everybody's Favorite)?... Each body she designed, then, was a body that her drivers could take as their own, and people could change their selves by changing what they drove. New immigrants to OZ could acquire the OZian Dream of assimilation by buying the forest-green or golden-rod Family Vans all families in OZ drove. Rebels could "fight the power" by buying flashy-red off-road vehicles. In either case they were beautiful products, and people made themselves beautiful by using them. And that was what she actually designed, beautiful people. A beautiful world.

In OZ, Fulfillment was as simple as the swipe of a charge card, Desire baroque as its codes.

CHAPTER FIVE

One day in IN, Mechanic was lying in sludge beneath a car, utility lamp tight in his teeth, when something within him snapped. No sooner had he gotten the filthy-black underbelly of the car unbuttoned than he found himself staring into the gleam of silver gears, radiant with honey-gold lubricant. Though he had seen gears like this thousands of times before, it had never once occurred to him how eloquently their polished metal teeth explained his life: their mesh and power ratios may as well have been engineers, and foundry men, all on a shaft, with machinists, and mechanics, as his father had been, and the farmers and cooks, as his mother had been, who fed the factory workers, and highway builders who made it possible for everyone to get to jobs that brought into existence the need for marvels such as cars which needed transmissions which needed gears which needed him. So intense was the wonder caused by this glimpse at the world and his place in it that Mechanic couldn't have been more agape had he been the fish that spends its life completely ignorant of "sea" until it found itself pitched gasping onto the beach, or a child, who upon overturning a rock and finding grubs reducing a rotten apple to dirt is able to think for the fist time, "That apple is I." It was as if he stumbled upon one of those forces which guide equally the planets in their orbits and the flight of an arrow—a force that had been there all along, making the visible what it was, though the force itself remained invisible, unspeakable, unrecognizable. Until now.

Trembling, and not knowing what else to do, he repaired the transmission and bolted it shut.

But as time went on, it became increasingly difficult for him to forget about what he had seen. Standing before customers who tried to describe the vapor lock plaguing their cars by making a hacking cough, or customers who, with the erudition of medieval peasants on the topic of thermodynamics, explained to Mechanic the symptoms of a slack timing chain by imitating a spastic tic, he came to understand that the ignorant sought him out not for enlightenment but solely to make the profound inner workings of Auto invisible: to fix whatever rattle or misfire or stall it was that had brought some offending fuel pump or brake drum or other mechanism before him so that he could return it to the dark and they could go on being fish who wouldn't think about the sea until it broke again.

Perhaps it was the continual barking of the dogs that finally got to him. Or the continual whine of tires on the toll-road bridge that the man lived troll-like below. The neighbors blamed it on the strain he had been under during the prolonged dying of first his father, then his mother, both from the unrelenting ugliness of the steel mills and oil refineries, and the endless barrel and crate and gunpowder and acetylene factories that permeated IN, and so permeated its citizen-employees, filling first their souls, then their lungs with a rust-colored stain. In any case, Mechanic found he could no longer go on as he had. He reached the point where he couldn't even pretend he cared if the autos left in his care were ever set "right." The street rodders and kustom kar rebuilders who came to him were a catalyst in this, escaping into their fantasies of chrome oil pans and black-lit leafsprings, air-brushed tattoo-art of virgins on hoods, skulls in the doorjambs, bodies so beautiful that they made the essence of Auto completely invisible.

Indeed, fitting a chromed manifold onto a gold-plated block, he began to be weighted down by his own culpability, his own—yes, moral sell out was not too strong a word.

So the next time a customer brought in a transmission for repair, he unbolted it from the chassis where it hung bat-like in darkness beneath the car. Then he remounted it upside down. Now, the gear shift lever which had previously stuck up between the bucket seats inside the car protruded from the car's underbelly

— ◍ —

while the gears themselves were exposed on the inside of the car where they were all quite visible, dangerously visible, to both driver and passengers.

"What the hell!" shouted the owner of the car upon his return.

Their argument ended with Mechanic throwing his customer out, keys after, the man's oaths to bring lawyers raining down confused by the wild snarling of the dogs flinging themselves against their pen to get at him.

A brief lexicon of words useful in IN: Blood Sausage. Carcinogenic. Steam Pipe.

CHAPTER SIX

Fenders flowed from her Conté crayon so fluidly that without even trying, Designer could doodle out a decade's worth of auto designs so that when thumbed in flip-book fashion, their tail fins would shrink, a Dimetrodon evolving into a salamander, before growing back into dinosaur-sized scale. Advanced Marketing loved her. But she herself began to feel as if there was something hollow, something missing in her sketches. And therefore in her life. As others in her office sat at their desks, their heads inside the Virtual Reality Helmets that let them try out 3-D visions of the autos she designed, she drifted away on the clouds, allowing herself to become lost in the elevator music that played continually in her corporately-sleek office.

    As every architect knows, the taller a building becomes, the more of its interior must be dedicated to elevators and their cables and lifting apparatus. And in order to make The Essence of OZ Building the tallest in the world, and thereby have it speak superiority over all other companies and their "second rate" skyscrapers, it had been necessary to devote the entire interior of this building to elevators. The hallways were elevators, the closets were elevators, the stairwells were elevators, the elevators were elevators, of course, but so were all of the offices, and Designer and the others who worked in these offices spent their days gliding up and down, serenaded by elevator music as they sat motionless at their desks, gunning engines and roaring around the room in virtual-reality cars, or applying the formulas that would spinoff last season's style into next year's must-have rage.

In OZ, there has never been a romantic comedy that was not This Season's Funniest Tender Movie!

CHAPTER SEVEN

Art had nothing to do with it. Even after one lawyer accused him of that crime, Mechanic maintained that art had nothing to do with what he did. It was simply that having grasped the essence of Car, he could no longer participate in the lie that was Not-Car, the lie that blindered people from the beauty of the Truth that resided beneath the false beauty they mindlessly used to tool about their work-a-day lives. And if making them see meant making their cars inoperable, in the way that a hammer was most itself when broken, so be it.

He had come to that realization the time one of his own hammers broke while he was using it to beat the fender of a customer's car into a shape that could never be taken for granted again. During his entire life he had taken that hammer for granted, even though it was the one true heirloom he had inherited from his father's

— ⓪ —

father's father, by way of his father's father, via his father. When he needed to tap free a cotter pin, he would reach for the hammer without even thinking, use it, then return it to its place with no more notice than he would give his lungs during a breath. But once the hammer broke, he saw that it was only when broken that he missed it, sorely missed it, which is to say, see its hammerness for what it was. And so it was with his?—

The next customer who called it "Art" had brought in a car with a leaky radiator. When he returned at the appointed hour to retrieve his automobile and stood before it, staring at the radiator, now in the space that normally held the windshield, Mechanic reached behind to his workbench and gripped his broken hammer in case he had to fight the man off. Too many times before, what should have been a simple exchange of payment for car keys turned into a scene of bewilderment, even rage. The dogs had learned to sense strong emotion and were already going wild in their cage, so this time Mechanic was ready.

What he thought was a growl gradually became a hissing—what?—laughter? Was the man laughing at his work? Mechanic could feel anger draw him to the fight. Come on, come on, he thought, just waiting for the man to turn on him with his fists. He might have let him have it right there from behind if the man hadn't been so much more frail than himself: bony shoulders, scrawny neck, a bald spot shining out through a head of long white hair. When the man finally did turn to Mechanic, though, he said, "You, sir, are a genius."

— ① —

Mechanic tightened his grip on the hammer.

Wiping pale, blue eyes, the man continued, "All my life I have driven this car without once considering the beauty, and functionality of its radiator, a metal honeycomb tirelessly cooling my auto's engine in summer, supplying heat to comfort my body in winter. But now I shall never drive again without first appreciating its handiwork, and yours, and all of those whose labor has helped make my locomotion and comfort possible. All my life I have longed for another who would understand, who could understand, the true beauty of art, and the world, instead of those lies and illusions we are expected to live by, and now, having discovered a single honest man, I feel I can die at peace."

Needless to say, whatever name the force goes by that reunites the salmon with its place of birth, that allows migrating ducks to hold their V; whatever marries sound to moving pictures, or print to page, had also brought together Mechanic and this man. Indeed, even before this meeting, they learned, they had been next-door neighbors, though not in the usual dimension. For this man, a Photographer, lived in a house that doubled as a camera and was built on the highest point of IN, the top of the bridge that sutured IN to OZ, the very bridge that Mechanic lived beneath. Mechanic, for his part, was shocked to learn that someone lived above him. Having spent his entire life under this bridge, hearing the decrescendo of tires as cars slowed to pay the toll that was required at its midpoint, then the crescendo of tires as those cars before sped off again, the sound had been a kind of nature to

— ⓪ —

him, the way the rhythmic rush, then hiss of waves must sound to villagers who live out their days beside an ocean. Learning that his sky contained a man couldn't have been more startling had he been a tourist eating a hotdog at a bathing beach when Venus rose from its sea.

After these successive shocks—first the shock of seeing clearly the essence of car, then the shock of discovering that the sky contained a man, he began to notice a lot of things he never had before. Like the dogs. Whenever a fight broke out between him and a customer, the dogs invariably took his side. That is, they were loyal to him, he saw, though he had never done anything to earn their loyalty, and this realization filled him with memories of his dead parents. As though waking from an emotional hibernation, he began to miss them, then human companionship in general, which he had become estranged from since their burials. When Photographer began dropping by, inviting Mechanic for a drink in one or another of the standard bars that dotted IN, he began to understand that this was what humans did. Then he began to take the initiative himself, calling on Photographer in his camera-house on the top of the toll bridge, and it felt right. Better than being alone. Seated there, guest-beer in hand, he'd gaze upon the Essence of OZ Building, shimmering mirage-like in the distance as Photographer went on about his own life, and loves, and of course his work.

Once he had been a film maker, Photographer said on one of these occasions. But the artificiality of time in films had sickened him, as did the relentless march of film through a projector, always in the same direction, and always moving at a speed that made it impossible for a person to truly see.

"So I started making films that consisted of only one frame," he said. "But audiences howled, 'These aren't films! They're photographs!'" Photographer spat out the window at the stream of cars passing beneath his house on the roadway of the bridge. "Philistines! Lemmings! Never did they say, this is a *bad* film. Never do they tell you, this is the work of a *bad* mechanic. Am I right? No! Instead they howl this *isn't* a film! Or this *isn't* a mechanical repair! Am I right? Am I right?"

Mechanic always felt humbled by Photographer's learning and ability to seize on the precise essence of a problem.

"So all right," Photographer continued, "I am but one man. They are the world. Yet rather than acquiesce to the making of what proctologists, accountants, and cheerleaders on Friday-night dates *opined* to be 'art,' I gave up films completely and began making photographs. For a while, I took great joy in looking through the viewfinder, changing the world by the way it was framed. I fell under the spell of framing. Believing as I did at that time that the essence of photography lay in the selection of what was left out, I began to experiment with ever-smaller frames, seeing more by including less until not even a microscope sufficed as lens. Looking through one at a hair on a gnat's ass—a tree, not the forest, so to speak—I came to see how even this was a forest of atoms. That is, I saw how the photos themselves, the mere flotsam of looking, were what most people wanted in a photograph while the photos were the very thing that arrested looking. So I began to take pictures without any film in the camera, which was finally satisfying, and led to this," he said, indicating the house around them: a walk-in camera obscura which focused light on a point where Photographer would stand, eyes shut, letting the image that came in through the window that was a lens project itself onto his closed eyelids.

CHAPTER EIGHT

Before coming to work in the Essence of OZ Building, Designer had never really listened to elevator music, so wouldn't even pretend to the level of connoisseurship shared by co-workers who argued the ornaments of every piece. But now that she found herself exposed to it during most of her waking hours, she felt captivated by it. Or at least captivated by the music that played in the elevator she worked in, which was more ethereal, more—different—than the music she had heard in other elevators.

The tempo changed, catching her off guard again, and as per the game she played against herself during her morning jogs, she turned down the next dirt road, pleasantly surprised to find a Technicolor rainbow over amber waves of grain undulating in the breezeless air.

If she guessed that the tempo would quicken, she

thought, picking up her pace to stay with the new pace of the music, it would suddenly stop; if other songs went *da-da-de*, this music would go simply *dada*. So intriguing were its departures that trying to anticipate them became as engrossing to her as soap opera or video games were to others.

It did it again—*Nuts!*—and she took another fork in the road, the waves of grain giving way to an arid, Road-Runner/Coyote terrain, a greeting-card sunrise enflaming spacious skies.

She understood why the self-proclaimed connoisseurs of elevator music she worked with dismissed it as they did, crying out, "This isn't elevator music!" It *was* different. Still, she had no counter argument. In previous disagreements, she always maintained that while she didn't know anything about music, she knew what she liked. But this—not even that reason applied to this music. For how could she claim to know what she liked when it demonstrated note by note that a person couldn't like what they didn't know?

The sun peeked through a purple mountain's majesty just as her jog took her by Mt. Rushmore, the gigantic stone heads of once-upon-a-time presidents having been replaced by bas-reliefs of the Excita, Bellvu, K9 and K7—the Company's four best sellers, cars and trucks that she had designed. Hearing that new, fluid music while seeing the sun glare with the baldness of an interrogation lamp on her old ideas, all set in stone, she couldn't help but feel as if the music was calling on her to explain. To justify....

Those designs, immortalized in stone for their popularity and sales, were not her best work she knew. She'd been young when she'd come up with them and now, older, more mature as a designer, the roof lines and trunk profiles she drew carried far more authority, even gravitas, and they showed her earlier designs for what they were: pirouettes on a high-wire by a girl too young and green to know let alone care about any musty burden of design history. Yet the more eloquent her designs became, speaking more while saying less, the fewer the people there were who seemed to get their depth. The fewer the people there were who *could* get it, she feared, an appreciation of her designs increasingly requiring as they did a knowledge of fender history, of the history of roof lines, of the limits and possibilities of sheet-metal bend-radii and injection-mold tensile strength and a million other technical constraints.... Though the reviewers for *Auto Times* and other culture magazines loved the layers of her work, though the speeches to stockholders and PR within the company alibied away the downturn on the charts for her models—citing cost-cutting measures, and budgets for billboards and cycles in the grease industry, the aging of their Sports Hero Spokesman, consolidation in container shipping or the movement of other stars— she herself couldn't silence the tiny voice that whispered from her pillow at night, "Could forty million auto buyers all be wrong?"

Oh What a Beautiful Morning began playing: the signal that the work day was about to begin and that the roads she'd been jogging down would in a few moments be taken over by cars racing through their

— ⓪ —

test laps. For an instant she had an intimation of waking up as she increasingly did at home, bolting upright in a sweat from a nightmare in which she had been reading her own name on a tombstone. Yet, pulling off the VR helmet to return to the fluorescent lighting and her work-a-day thoughts here in the office, she somehow found solace in this strange elevator music—this music with its synthesizers and discords and who-knows-what that was complex beyond comprehension but could, nevertheless, be felt by someone like her who didn't know a thing about music. And when she looked beyond her art book on the windowsill and out toward the sun rising dully over the brown stain on the horizon that was IN, she couldn't help but feel that there was some answer that she wasn't seeing. Something beyond OZ that she knew nothing about.

In OZ, flowers are always delivered hermetically sealed in plastic.

CHAPTER NINE

The gravity that had brought Mechanic and Photographer together continued its tide pull and soon Mechanic was moving within Photographer's current of friends, including one Composer who had become, like Photographer's other friends, a friend of Mechanic as well. So, when a tragedy befell Composer, Mechanic didn't need to be told that he and Photographer would go sit shiva with him, to be there, to help, though there was nothing they could actually do.

They took Mechanic's car, a large sedan that an irate customer had abandoned after he failed to see why Mechanic had welded its wheels to the roof, and mounted car doors like skis where there used to be wheels. Night falling, security lights with the brightness of arc welders began to wink on above the sheds and backdoors they protected. As Mechanic and

Photographer pushed the car through their neighborhood of concrete houses and sludge-compacting plants, its eventide serenity, the evensong of its buzzing security lights was broken only by their grunts of exertion, and the occasional roar of smoke stacks venting fireballs of burning waste gas.

I ASSUME YOU DRIVE EXCITA? said one soot-streaked billboard, a sophisticated woman in a bikini tuxedo splayed across the hood of a new pickup truck.

Looking down was easy in IN; though its streets had no lamps, the number of sheds and backdoors and front doors and barred windows that sported a full-sized streetlight to deter break-ins was so great that it was never dark. But to look up, to see higher than the billboards, or to see where they were going, Mechanic had to shield his eyes, the huge lamps that were intended to be mounted twenty-five feet above the pavement always glaring at eye-level like intense bug zappers that killed the night and its stars. They gave the deserted streets the silvery cast of dead fish, and the color often made Photographer remark that living in IN was like living in an eternal black-and-white photo, an Atget (whatever that was).

It stayed that way until the cramped streets of worker houses and sulfur mills and loading docks and slag heaps and munitions factories began to give way to blocks with huge gaps in them. The outline of a foundation marked where a standard school had recently stood. Other lots were empty except for square silhouettes of the standard houses that had

— ⓪ —

filled them before that neighborhood's oil refinery blew up, taking the neighborhood with it. This was also the point where the river that snaked through IN had caught fire back when Mechanic was just a kid. Its stagnant water had become such a cocktail of chemical runoff from the industrial plants along its banks that its very nature changed, like those dead, salt-saturated seas that eventually make rocks float, this river having become flammable.

Since he had grown up under a bridge, he had gotten to know most of the firefighters of IN, bridges affording the most convenient spots from which to spray the flaming river with their chemical foams. Some of those original firefighters were now reaching retirement age—the ones who hadn't been burnt alive in the initial days—and every time Mechanic came across one of those strapping young men—giants in his child's mind—now graying and frail, having spent their lives fighting the river, he felt a poignant tenderness toward them. Toward every mortal creature.

Years ago they had switched to fire hoses in the hopes that spraying water on the river would have the double benefit of returning it to its mostly aquatic, pre-flammable state, and the plan had mostly worked. Unlike the first weeks when Mechanic and his family had been evacuated to live with other families in an unused civic theater, firefighters now only had to be called out to control the occasional spot blaze. It was considered easy duty so given to those old timers who had been there through the worst.

— ◉ —

Mechanic recognized one of them on a pumper in the distance, languidly working the spray from its hose over a patch of smoldering water and he honked the horn of his car in greeting. The firefighter waved the spray up and down in reply.

The landscape was charcoal black from the recent refinery fire, though—except for a scattering of shiny-new billboards that rose from its crust like the first, new green shoots after a forest conflagration.

ALIVE WITH PLEASURE! silently proclaimed a boisterous tableau of young, athletic, cigarette smokers. A second, circular billboard had been erected before it, painted black with yellow swirls that made it look like the vortex of a sewer, or a toilet, swirling with distort-ed words that were being sucked in. The words were stretched out so much by the vortex that it was impos-sible for Mechanic and Photographer to read them until they reached a point where they had an edge-on view of the billboard and the elongated letters were foreshortened enough to leap into clarity:

It was the work of a group of poets who thought they could fight the general abstinence from thought that plagued IN by convincing its electorate to limit the number of billboards, which to them were nothing more than a cancer of canned thought, a kind of anti-poetry. Photographer had told Mechanic the whole story on the way to one of their committee meetings: how once the anti-billboard faction managed to get the limitations of billboards on the ballot as a referendum, the pro-billboard faction began to wage their own public relations campaign, erecting even more billboards to beautify the countryside with mountain-sized pictures of autumn in Vermont or Niagara Falls or ☺s that would cheer people, make them feel good about themselves, and of course, about billboards. Though the poets had won the first battle, they realized that they were losing the war and that their only hope was in fighting fire with fire, i.e., billboards. Billboards were, after all, the single most efficient means by which to reach drivers, those voters most likely to care about the issue. And if *poets* couldn't defeat language whores with words, well then, there was no hope for anyone. An arms race of billboards ensued, with each side writing in the gaps between the signs of the other with ever bigger and more conspicuous billboards. It wasn't going well for the poets. And yet, though the committee meeting that Photographer had insisted Mechanic attend with him had grown very heated—fistfights prickled the proceedings—Photographer had remained surprisingly calm. Mechanic couldn't imagine why until afterwards Photographer scrambled around the upturned chairs and after-meeting arguments to introduce Mechanic to one of the poets who was leaving. A woman poet.

Or maybe she was a Sculptor. Mechanic could never be sure since Poet (or Sculptor) no longer made any work. She had been so disgusted, Photographer had explained on the way home (or maybe she had been enamored—again, Mechanic had never been sure which), by the ease of reading billboards, by their commanding presence in the world—language embodied—and by their enormous audiences that she took them to their logical conclusion, adopting dirt as her medium, dirt being, of course, the most democratic of all mediums. And since dirt covered all the earth, there was no need for her to make any other poems (sculptures), there being nothing more to say (see).

"...such an intelligent, and sensitive woman, don't you think?" Photographer said now, the sight of the billboards they passed having given him reason to bring her up again. He brought her up a lot, it seemed. And each time it was to sound Mechanic out for his opinion of the woman. Or so it seemed. And he talked about her in a way that Mechanic never heard him talk of anyone: tenderly. What was between them? Mechanic wondered, considering that Photographer was old enough to be her father. But he kept his peace, pushing in silence as the last of the town petered out, becoming a dark and empty plain.

"Ah, we've arrived," Photographer said.

They shouldered the car onto the shoulder of the road, blocked the steering wheel with a large metal bar and padlock, then walked the last several hundred

— ⓪ —

yards across a vast, vacant site up to where Composer lived: a deep shaft, created by the quarrying of granite used for the skin of the Essence of OZ Building and which, therefore, was that building's inverse image, as deep as the Essence of OZ Building was high, and with its exact shape. Locals knew it as The Essence of IN Hole.

Solemnly, out of respect for the Composer's grief, they descended. As expected, they found him at the bottom of the hole, bereft and supine on a fainting couch. Someone, he had discovered, had been playing his music. Not the way it was meant to be played, no, for it could in fact not be played at all: as his work matured, he had found himself increasingly impatient with the constraints all composers were forced to work under: the fact, for instance, that a violinist only had two arms. For a while he had tried to work around these constraints, creating compositions that required two violinists to man a single instrument so that the second musician could supply, when necessary, the extra fingers required by his music. But eventually even this became to him a form of suffocation, an impossible straight-jacketing of his ideas. So he abandoned what he had come to see as the ultimate constraint in music— hearing—and he began to compose only for those who read music, those who could play his music in their minds by looking at the notes he wrote for trumpets with as many keys as a saxophone, flutes that could be appreciated in the audio-bound world only by dogs, or harps with strings so long that their subsonic reverberations could be felt only by whales far out at sea, and for the first time in his life he breathed free.

Only now, he had learned, someone in OZ had figured out a way to use computers and other electronics to play his inaudible music, and was playing it everywhere. Even in elevators. And the news couldn't have been more devastating to him had he learned that a beloved child had been transformed into a zombie, a grotesque parody of his darling, and loosed upon the world to serve as his representative and stand-in for the real Music, true Music, the Music he actually composed and in which the world showed absolutely no interest.

CHAPTER TEN

In Oz, Mental Health is measured by The Index of Economic Indicators.

MUSSIKAL INC., was listed under artistic credits in the maintenance log of the elevator that Designer worked in. MUSSIKAL INC. Standing in her office at night, she gazed out at the dots of fire that snaked through IN. For it was exactly like that—Musical ink—indelible as the ink of a tattoo writing itself upon her, the tickle of its needle making her shiver. And where there was a tattoo, she knew, there had to be a tattoo artist.

CHAPTER ELEVEN

To cheer their comrade, Mechanic and Photographer decided to mount a concert of Composer's music so that the world could hear it the way it was meant to be heard, that is, in silence. So they rented an alternative performance space, i.e., one of the many abandoned warehouses of IN, and they printed up handbills:

World Premier

One Night Only

A Performance of

"The Essence of Music"

presented so that the world can hear for

itself the difference between True Music

and the bastard children masquerading

— ① —

as the Real and True Music, a grotesquerie of Honesty, a saccharine TRAVESTY of HOW THINGS ARE which distorts not by lying but by FRAMING the world in such a way so as to CROP from view the WHOLE OF MUSIC and make of it a standardized assemblage of sounds to play while in the car or vacuuming the house, The Lap Dog of Muisakal Inc. and all its Movie-TV-Satellite-Theme Park-Action Figure-Billboard-Toilet Seat-Coffee Bean-Shower Curtain Subsidiaries, the darling of the corporate culture newsletter—a.k.a. *The Daily Times*—giving Customers (a.k.a. Readers) what they want—50,000 Shareholders can't be wrong!

— FAMILY RELATIONS! SENTIMENT! HIGH SCHOOL MEMORIES! EPIPHANIES!—

faceless, nameless, ubiquitous mUSic valorized for its vanquishing of elitism, its glorification of The Common Man and The Common Woman and their place on the Common Assembly Line and the power it gives him AND her to assert their SELVES by BUYING OUR PRODUCT. Listen to it now and again and you'll discover the Miracle of LOVE. And so convenient it can be turned on or off like a FAUCET....

Since Photographer had composed the fine print, it ranted for several pages, comprising as it did a kind of manifesto.

On the night of the performance, Mechanic manned the enormous scrolling contraption he had cobbled together from junkyard parts and abandoned circus equipment: a huge canvas scroll powered by a 600 h.p. diesel engine that roared when he shifted gears to make the canvas gradually unwind like the roll of a player piano as it crossed the stage. At the rear of the warehouse, Photographer manned a movie projector, lying on its side so that as the scroll unwound from one spool to the other, the pages of sheet music that Photographer had photographed then spliced together to form a continuous movie would be projected upon the blank canvas of the unscrolling scroll, in synch with it.

Composer sat in the front row of the dozen folding chairs they had set up. There was no one else in the audience, save Poet (Sculptor). Mechanic could tell that this was a special occasion for her by the way she'd gotten dressed up. Though she wore the same battleship gray factory uniform she'd had on at the anti-billboard meeting, the tails of its work shirt were tucked in. She'd also buttoned the top button of her shirt in a formal sort of way. She sat politely waiting, feet flat on the floor, knees together, her hands clasped around a Mason jar full of dirt in her lap. To amuse her, Mechanic revved the engine and worked the clutch; Photographer held a palm against the film's rotating take-up reel to adjust its speed, the two of them tuning like a violinist and cellist.

— ⓪ —

Then they were ready.

In the idle before the first downbeat, the slamming boom of warehouse doors echoed throughout the cavernous metal building. A woman appeared—a woman in a smart, white-satin business suit. She strode toward them like a fashion model on a runway, hips and shoulders swiveling in sync, her high-heels clicking loudly across the concrete floor. She held a tiny, white lap-dog that shivered from the damp of the leaky warehouse/auditorium, cowering as she swung it onto her lap to take a seat in the audience.

Throttle open. The diesel engine roared deafeningly. The projector flickered to life, bringing up the first bars of the projected music. In the glow, Mechanic could see Composer following the music with his eyes, his face a portrait of a man gazing out into the rarefied air of a mountain he had tried to scale all his life. Though Mechanic was occupied with running the scroll, shifting gears to speed it up at the fast parts of the music, slowing it down when the notations said *deselerando,* the engine roared continually, reverberating so loudly in the otherwise empty warehouse that the floor shook. Through it all, Composer sat transfixed, and Mechanic was touched to see how moved Composer obviously was by the kindness his friends had performed for him: he seemed to be living and dying by turns as the music took ecstatic flight or plunged into somber depths. Often, he would bite his knuckles, barely able to watch, or clasp his hands prayerfully as a particularly moving passage was projected to wall-size. Poet (Sculptor) also concentrated with the attention of one learning a new language, squinting to follow the notations.

The other woman sat stupefied, her hands clamped over the ears of the dog in her lap. As the overture progressed, her head swiveled from Mechanic operating the scroll, to Photographer operating his projector behind as if she were passing an auto accident and didn't know whether to gawk at the mangled wreckage on the highway or the bodies in the ditch. They had nearly reached the one hour mark when she finally let go of the dog and put her fingers in her own ears against the roar of the engine. Then as the second measure began, she cradled her head in her hand. Mechanic was glad she was sitting behind Composer so he couldn't see her inattention. He was glad she was in front of the projector so that Photographer couldn't see that half of the audience was such a— Such a— Yes, there was no denying the word—such a philistine. Though he couldn't follow most of the music himself, he understood the undivided attention it required, while she had given up on following it so completely that she was grooming her dog—a visual equivalent to the elderly who leave their hearing aids at home, then thinking the music has ended, begin talking loudly over the soft passages of a symphony.

Why had she come, Mechanic wondered, traveling to a neighborhood that was obviously worse than her own? Her lips formed a perfect Cupid's bow and were painted red, her suit so tailored to her body that it could not have come off of any of the standard racks of IN. Compared to the grays and browns that dominated IN, her sleek white suit made her a gleaming new Ferrari to their graveyard of discarded washtubs, and he couldn't stop stealing glances at her. Two hours later, when the music hit a lengthy passage that was all in third gear, he was able to prop the throttle in a fixed position and leave his stool. She obviously hadn't known to come prepared, so he walked past Poet (Sculptor) and went to her and, in the deafening drone, offered by way of gestures for her to take half of the sandwich he had brought for his own dinner. She shook her head, mouthing the words NO THANK YOU, and he was struck by how gracious she was, even in refusal, as though it didn't matter that she was there in a perfect white suit, perfect blonde hair while he was a pile of mechanic's weeds, the whiteness of his sandwich bread accentuating his tool-blackened fingernails.

Her dog stared at the sandwich. Using gestures again, he offered to give it to him, and again by mouthing the words with lips so red and full that they seemed to move in slo-motion, she said he was too kind. But after he vehemently asserted that he didn't mind, she acquiesced, and he gave it over. Perched back on his stool, again in control of the throttle, he ate his own half of the sandwich. The dog had already finished, and was sniffing around the base of her chair, licking up crumbs. Mechanic resolved to stop staring at the woman, but as the concert drove on, she made looking at her increasingly easy, her eyelids growing heavy, drowsily closing for longer and longer periods. Finally her head nodded down to her chest. When her dog reared its hinnie, he was glad she was asleep so she couldn't see it crap on the warehouse floor.

Seven hours later, as the last few bars of music were projected on the scroll, he was only staring at her, slouched in her metal folding chair, her dog asleep in her lap, her own eyes shut too, her ears plugged with Kleenex against the roar of the engine.

In the front row, Composer was also limp, but from rapture. As the final note of the music played out across the screen, and in unison Photographer and Mechanic cut out the projector and engine, he sprung to his feet, applauding wildly. The woman awoke with a start. She looked around as though it took her a few moments to realize where she was. When she did, she also began to applaud. Mechanic and Poet (Sculptor) joined in, standing and clapping with Photographer shouting, "*Bravo! Bravissimo!*"

Weak with happiness, Composer struggled to stand. He stepped from the rows of folding chairs up to the front of the scroll, clasping his hands together and shaking them victoriously overhead in the manner of prize fighters, or opera conductors who redirect the applause meant for them back to the orchestra in the pit while Poet (Sculptor) presented him with her Mason jar of dirt, her bouquet. "My friends, my dear, dear friends," he announced, gesturing to Mechanic and Photographer when the applause finally died down. "Let me at least buy you a drink."

Mechanic, Photographer and Composer pulled

on their coats, and Poet (Sculptor) joined them as they headed for the door, each glancing back at the woman who only continued to stand near her seat, holding her dog.

"Who is she?" they asked one another, huddling, each having assumed she was one of the other's relatives.

Finally, Composer, still glowing with gratitude and love for his friends, and indeed, all humanity, bowed to the woman, and said, "Madam, my friends and I are going to a nearby tavern to celebrate this momentous occasion. You are more that welcome to join us."

"Yes," Mechanic told the woman, stepping in front of Poet (Sculptor) to do so. "You are more than welcome."

Outside, they offered her a ride, but since she had her own car, she said she would follow, then hurried off to get it, her dog taking quick steps to keep up.

"Hey," Photographer yelled, seeing that Poet (Sculptor) was about to ride away on her bicycle. "Aren't you coming?" he called, jogging to catch up to her.

In high spirits, Composer jumped onto the hood of Mechanic's car. "Va-ROOOOOM!" he yelled, calling to her that they had lots of room. Mechanic could see Photographer trying to convince Poet (Sculptor) to come with them, tugging her elbow toward the group in a kidding sort of way. In the end she kept shaking her head, and Photographer kissed her on the cheek, then rejoined the group alone.

"Your friend's not coming?" Mechanic asked, taking up a good position to push.

"You blockhead," Photographer answered, also putting a shoulder to the trunk.

"Huh?"

"Va-ROOOOM! Va-ROOM!" Composer roared from the hood, reaching in through its open windshield to steer. A white car, the woman in her car, pulled up behind them, and they were off. If there were ever any pedestrians in IN, which there never were, they might have mistaken Composer's va-rooming for the revving of the car's engine. But the woman, who drove close behind at their pedestrian's pace, immediately recognized the sound as an imitation of the engine that had powered his concert.

A light, oily mist began to fall, making the pushing easier and lifting spirits, and soon Mechanic stopped wondering why Photographer had been cross. As during the concert, he couldn't keep his eyes off of the woman—and her car: a white coupe bowed as an angel wing, or dolphin fin, or a cresting wave—it was impossible to say—it being a car such as never appeared in IN until years after its new-car smell had been consumed by the noses of previous owners.

Inside the bar, he continued to let her nearness etch itself on his mind as the others talked excitedly about the concert. Photographer, of course, critiqued his own, and Mechanic's interpretation, finding it far short of what the music deserved. He mused on future performances, and wished they had thought to attach a muffler to deaden the roar of the engine. Composer would hear none of it. Though normally reticent, he was still in high spirits and exuberantly claimed that the performance was just as he had always imagined. Better than he had imagined, for if the engine hadn't drowned out the noise of the street outside, and the drips from the ceiling inside, and the barking of the audience's dog, who knows what horrors of harmonics they might have combined into? "Perfect silence is very difficult to achieve," he noted, "and so sometimes one must settle for its equivalent, White Noise."

Though Mechanic had thought the woman hadn't seen a note, she spoke as knowledgeably about the music as any of them. Even passionately. She waxed poetic about how much the music meant to her personally, thanking Composer for bringing it into the world, the world being a more beautiful place for it. Her enthusiasm kindled their own and they all laughed and joked about the world, and art, with Photographer talking about looking, and Composer scribbling out songs on a napkin for their entertainment. All was as effervescent as the bubbles in their beer until there was a lull in the conversation and the woman turned to Mechanic and asked, "So what's wrong with your car?"

The question, the fact that she had spoken directly to him, brought him up short. "W-What do you mean?"

"Your car. What's wrong with it? Why does it have doors for wheels? And why are its wheels welded on top of its roof?"

"My friend is an artist," Photographer announced, lifting his beer in homage. "That car is his art."

The woman's angelic brow wrinkled. "Why?"

Photographer rolled his eyes as if she had asked the stupidest question he had ever heard and Mechanic kicked him under the table to tell him to let it go.

But the woman persisted. "I mean, I wouldn't want a car with its wheels on its roof. I wouldn't be able to drive to work. I live twenty miles from my job. Why don't you make cars people can drive to work?"

The table fell silent. Mechanic rocked his glass, making O-rings with its damp bottom, for truly, he couldn't say. Finally Photographer, who lived within a camera, said with what Mechanic thought was undue sarcasm, "Why don't you live closer to your work?"

"I just don't see why anyone would—"

"*Obviously*, he wants people to see that cars have wheels," Photographer said in a patronizing way, pronouncing the words slowly, as though for a child.

The woman was unfazed. "But everyone already knows that."

"And anyway," Photographer said, growing hotter by the moment, "what do you know about such matters?"

"A lot, actually. I design cars."

The table was struck dumb. Then Composer repeated, obviously impressed, "You are a designer of automobiles?" And the woman, Designer, explained how she worked in the Essence of OZ Building, designing the sleek molded bumpers that covered the shock absorbers that actually protected a car from bumps, and the gleaming facades of chrome spokes that hid the grotesque nuts that held the wheels to their axles. Composer asked many questions, drawing her out on every detail, their call and response growing into a festival of admiration. "So you too begin by composing in silence?" he said, when she explained how it all began with a blank sketch pad. Once the initial idea was down in black and white, as thought embodied, she next turned it into eye-candy, developing her ideas with pastels, fleshing out the sensual curves of poreless skin, massaging and massaging until the drawing looked like…. "Well, until it looked like your car," she told Mechanic.

"Y-You designed my car?" Mechanic stammered.

She nodded. "Before you put its wheels on its roof, that is."

Photographer, who had been sitting there scowling the whole while hugged Mechanic to him and snapped at her, "Well my friend here *fixed* your design!"

He and Composer began arguing heatedly, but Mechanic didn't hear, his mind stuck in the single gear of the woman before him designing his car. To think that first there was nothing. Then there was something! His own car! And it had come from her pen. It was no easier to get his mind around her, or anyone, dreaming his car into existence than it was to imagine a blacksmith forging a river. Yet here she was, and yes she had. A river goddess, bringing into existence not only the river but the banks it cut, the rocks it polished, the forests it watered, the trees it uprooted, the rapids it rode and the falls it plunged down along the way.

CHAPTER TWELVE

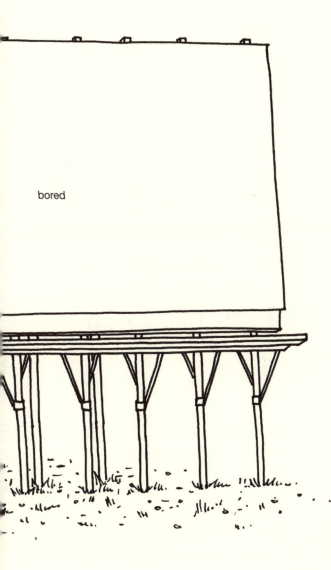

bored

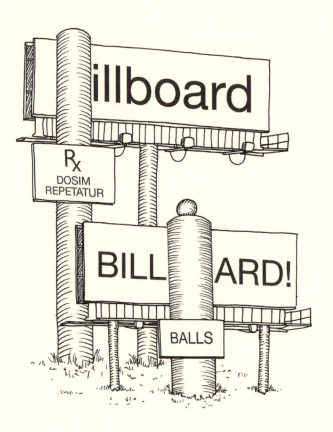

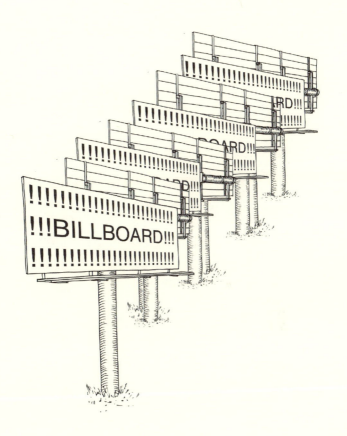

CHAPTER THIRTEEN

That night, Mechanic was too excited to sleep. Standing in the alley behind his garage, he understood the emotional release Photographer must have felt laying eyes on the radiator where his windshield used to be and recognizing the presence of a kindred spirit. If he and her could work together, he saw, more clearly than he had ever seen anything in his life, then he was sure they could come up with some way to make everyone not only be able to see what he had seen, but want to see it—as badly as he wanted her to—he wanted her—he wanted—

He bent back and let out a howl. This set off his dogs within the garage, and laughing he unlatched the door. The dogs burst out, ramming him to the ground with the force of an exploding acetylene tank. Before their teeth could break skin, though, they

— ⓪ —

recognized his smell and he instead found himself enveloped in licking tongues. He struggled back to his feet, simultaneously ruffling their fur, and kneeing the jumping dogs in the chest to keep them from knocking him down again. The exuberance of the happy dogs forced him to push them away harder, then punch them in the mouths. They continued to leap on him, and he continued to punch them till knuckles and mouths bleeding, he yelled, "Go on! Get out of here!" As if too shocked by their good fortune to move, the dogs needed a kick before they yelped, then tore off down the alley, barking ecstatically, and snapping at each other.

In bed, his mind raced with wild visions of all the fabulous devices he and Designer could invent together: automobiles with clear bodies so people could see the engines inside, and engines with clear blocks so people could see their pistons derricking up and down. Their autos would be like anatomical models on wheels: The Visible Man and also The Visible Woman, with red oil coursing through their veins, a colon of pink exhaust. On through the night he revised their dreams, the distant yapping of the dogs followed by the occasional clatter of garbage cans serenading him till tired and happy he fell asleep.

CHAPTER FOURTEEN

Poetry in OZ, which is generally sold in drugstores, is generally
printed on cardboard that can be folded to fit in envelopes.

In the morning, Designer arrived at her desk and began to sketch the idea she'd gotten driving through the wind at the top of the toll bridge she had to cross to get home. But every drawing she began resembled a pipe organ on wheels. She'd tear off a new page, then begin again, the idea whistling just beyond reach, just illusive enough to escape her crayon….

In general, poetry is not sold in IN.

CHAPTER FIFTEEN

Nights, Mechanic's furnace roared, its sides pulsing with a dark, blood-red heat. Each slam of the drop-forge it powered was another rhyme in the visual sonnet he was composing for her—*Wham! Wham!*—hammering crankcase bearings, and piston rods into pressed-flowers of themselves. As he worked, the enormous flywheel of his forge slowly rotated, its massive millstone of a counterweight adding enough danger to the garage to command respect from anyone for it and its unforgiving brute power, its indifference to whether it was crushing metal or bone.

Chewing a stump of jerky during a break, he considered the marks he already bore: a white, crescent-moon of a scar on one thumb from a brush against a hot manifold; skinned knuckles from the times a wrench he had been pushing hard against slipped its nut, a mechanic's occupation writing itself on his body, as it had on his father's—just as the fate of his watchdogs had been determined by their powerful bodies and jaws, just as the petite size of Designer's dog afforded it a place in her lap. And yet, he knew, spotting his broken hammer, his was a fate past, not future, and he smiled at the thought of the empty dog cage outside, even if his livelihood as a mechanic seemed to have left with them.

Initially, the dwindling customers made him doubt himself as a mechanic—could all of those car owners be wrong? He'd break out in an existential sweat trying to come up with an answer. For if he wasn't a mechanic, what was he? Like those hermits who had too much time on their hands for thinking about God, he might have lost his mind completely if he hadn't had Photographer there to convince him that the deeper he was within himself as a mechanic, the fewer people there would be who would want him to work on their cars: "What else did you expect?"

Not this, he admitted to himself once alone again. Not the continual fighting with customers. Seeing one after another desert him was too much like déjà vu of the solitude he was in after his parents died. Especially the day he repaired the car of an old friend of his father's: a friend that his father had known since the days when they worked in the plant together, long before Mechanic's father had become a mechanic; a friend so old and so much like family that Mechanic's father had worked on this friend's Standard Auto for years for free, keeping a car running that the two of

— ⓪ —

them had actually helped build as young men doing their bit as it went down the line and whose simple mechanisms Mechanic had continued to keep running ever since his father died—a link between them. When this old family friend had come around to pick up his vehicle after the last repair, though, he had stopped abruptly in the bay door of the garage, the two after-work cold-ones he'd brought by to ease reminiscing falling from his hands and shattering on the concrete floor of the garage as he stared at his car standing on end and sledge hammered into the shape of an Urn. Slowly, his eyes welled with tears. His head hung there with the limpness of a dead man walking. Then he turned and left without saying a word, too choked up to speak, and after he was gone, Mechanic slumped down onto his toolbox and wept.

He wept for his father and his father's friend, mourning the time when they were strapping young cock-o-the-walks in the plant. He wept for himself— for an innocent time when he was just a boy and had borrowed his father's tools to fix his own bicycle for the very first time. How happy he'd been! How proudly they had beamed at him!

His mood blackened. There was no going back. Even if he wanted to. He couldn't not know what he knew, no matter how badly he wished it. And knowing what he knew, he knew he could never wish it. No, not him. Not ever again.

So he concluded one day, trying to square his inner being with the loss of his outer business, If Thomas Alva Edison was a mechanic, he didn't want

— ⓪ —

to be a mechanic. If Archimedes was a mechanic, he didn't want to be a mechanic. If Da Vinci was a mechanic, he thought, he'd give it a chance. But he didn't need "customers" to do so—not if, as Photographer claimed, it was looking that made the photographer, or dancing the dancer.

Without giving it any more thought, he got up one morning, put on his mechanic's boots, and his mechanic's uniform, but instead of opening his shop, he walked past the empty dog pen, walked past the oil stains in the empty driveway where customers once lined up with their foul plugs, and blown gaskets. He got behind his own car and pushed it out onto the road, signaled for a U-turn, then began the long, arduous climb up the grade that became the bridge he lived beneath where up-above he took a job as a tollbooth attendant.

If he could no longer repair cars, truly repair them and not just make offending parts invisible, then he could at least appreciate them, and do his own work, the work no one would pay him to do, on his own time, as poets and philosophers have always done. Rather than participate in what had become for him unbearable, he would stand in a tiny booth at the middle of the bridge that connected the flat-land of IN with the floating world of OZ, midway between earth and sky, collecting tolls from the passing motorists while the planets aligned, and perhaps, the one audience who mattered the most came out to meet him half way. And so he did, seeing her hand in every sensuous fender, every perky headlamp and all

the quarter panels, door trim and the rest that ebbed,
then flowed through his lane.

In IN, Desire was as simple as stripes on a bar code, Fulfillment as
baroque as a loan.

CHAPTER SIXTEEN

"Composers who insist upon working within the audio spectrum," Composer said, "would do well to study that most perfect of concert instruments, the slide whistle." He, Mechanic, and Designer, but not Photographer, Photographer having refused to come along, were in one of the many industrial taverns of IN, smoking standard cigarettes, and drinking standard alcohol that tasted to Mechanic like antifreeze. He himself would have never chosen this tavern, which only went by the name DRINK BOOZE. Especially not as a place to meet such a non-standard woman as Designer. But the dirtier the bar, the more directly its income was tied to the factory payroll, the more Composer and Photographer seemed to like it. He had always dismissed this aspect of their taste as just another of the many things he didn't understand about them. But it became especially baffling when he learned that Composer and Photographer had both been born in OZ and educated in OZ and still had the money to live in OZ, their families made up of wealthy OZ professors and business people, even doctors and judges—a fact he should have realized from the first time they shook hands, their hands being as soft as the foam rubber of luxury-car seats. Unlike his own standard mechanic's hands. Or the hands of his mechanic father. Or the hands of his mother who had to carry heavy pots of cabbage every day of her life. Or, come to think of it, the hands of everyone he had ever known growing up in IN. This legacy of hands was why he, but neither of them, was concerned about finding actual work. That is, the kind of work that was dull and/or dirty and/or dangerous and/or demeaning and so no one wanted to do and would therefore pay to have done for them, unlike making music or art—what they also called their "work." But it didn't explain why they had chosen to live in IN, while he, if he had ever thought of it which he never did, it being such an impossible thing to think, would have liked to live in OZ.

"Listening to the slide whistle," Composer was saying, "we understand how illusory are the borders of any single 'note.' We understand how it is only through an appeal to the most artificial of conventions, the musical score, the constraints of hearing, that the composer of the audio spectrum makes us come to believe in this sleight-of-hand called music." He paused to take a slow

— ◍ —

drag on his cigarette, letting the smoke whistle out. "A-sharp or B-flat?"

Mechanic couldn't help but notice how Designer hung on his words. Dressed down in a faux work shirt tailored to show off her figure, her hair was pulled back under a matching stoker's cap. It accentuated the clean design of her face—square chin and a model's cheekbones. Stealing glances at her foreign-import proportions, he could distinguish through her dungarees the outline of leggy legs, as sleek and elegant as her own designs. One leg dangling over the other, they ended in shoes designed to resemble work boots only not so much that it wouldn't be obvious that she didn't actually "work" (in the way the word was used in IN); her faux work boots were too petite to contain the steel reinforcing that real boots needed to protect toes from being crushed by a dropped beam. Even if her work shirt had had her name stitched over its pocket like a real work shirt instead of the "Grrrr-l" that was actually embroidered there, even if she wore greasy coveralls, the bar patrons gawking at her could have told she wasn't from IN, Mechanic knew, Mechanic being one of them.

He considered his own pin-striped mechanic's coveralls. Then he considered the pipe-fitter's jacket and turtleneck Composer wore. Though they both bought their clothes at the same resale and vintage boutiques of gas-station attendant uniforms and high-voltage-proof hip-waders, the work shirts that Mechanic wore looked like work shirts, while Composer's work shirts somehow came off as fashion. Why? Mechanic wondered, looking from the lifetime of premium, not standard, health benefits written in the luster of Designer's blonde hair, to the straightness and whiteness of Composer's teeth, to both of their creamy-smooth skins: skin that looked perpetually new unlike repainted hoods and fenders that always showed a trace, especially when the light was right, of earlier crumples that could never be hammered out completely.

"Aesthetic decisions have real-world consequences," Composer said, speaking up to be heard over the argument growing around one of the standard coin-operated pool tables found in all the bars of IN. "By preventing audiences from slipping into the passive, dreamlike trance of listening, by forcing them to instead work for every note with their eyes, they apprehend the constructed nature of music. That is, as they follow one of my scores, they see how there is nothing natural about it—or any music. March music, for example. While our passions are being excited by the rhythms of march music, its stirring melodies of fifes, bugles, and drums, we also absorb, usually unconsciously, how natural it is for there to be a military to play it."

One of the guys playing pool was a sinewy rat of a sheet-metal worker, sheet-metal workers always having massive forearms from scissoring their shears through tin all day but not the biceps that come from heavy lifting. His partner, the big guy, was a jackhammer operator with a paunch like all jackhammer operators developed to help absorb recoil. It flattened against the pool table when he leaned in to take a shot. The two of them were playing Dunk-a-Drunk

8-Ball, so whoever lost had to chug a shot of standard whiskey. The jackhammer operator was losing. And the more he lost, the drunker he got, the more he lost, the drunker he got, the more he lost & Etc. Every time he threw back another drink, his wiry opponent took the opportunity to chalk a fingertip with one of the blue cubes meant for the cues. Then he would say, "That's using the noggin," and stamp a blue dot on the big guy's ugly forehead.

"Listen," Composer said. He whistled a single tone. Following his lead, Designer puckered in silent whistle, her lips so wet and full that Mechanic's limbs weakened. "Is this note high or low?" Composer asked. He answered his own question by shrugging. "Impossible to say, of course, unless we compare it to the previous note. Or the note that will follow. But are those notes high or low? Soon we are comparing them to all sound." He pushed back the asbestos helmet liner he wore as a beret. "When we do, we see how illusory is the concept of 'a' note. There can be no 'note' without an absence of sound between other sounds. No downbeat without an upbeat, no beat at all without silence. And so it is with all genres of music and the invisible assumptions that make them possible: No military music without a military. No church music without a history of churches. No...."

The losing pool player wiped his brow and his hand came away a sweaty, blue smear just as he spotted the rat-guy chalking his fingertip for another strike. Like some hulking beast with a nervous system too primitive to immediately register pain, he looked from his blue-streaked hand, to the other player, chalk in hand, then to his own blue hand again. He rubbed more blue chalk from his face, stared at the confirmation. Then he exploded. Rat-man broke for the door but the hulk blocked his escape, stepping into the aisle between the pool table and the standard cigarette machines that lined the wall.

He snapped off the end of his pool cue by hitting it against the table.

Rat-man's grin vanished. He sprung onto the table, ran its length then leapt for the door. Just as he left his feet, his opponent stabbed him in the stomach with the jagged end of the stick. Women shrieked. He seemed to freeze in mid-air, his disbelieving eyes big as cue balls staring down at the spear protruding from his gut. Clutching it, he collapsed face-up on the table. Other patrons raced to his writhing figure. Some produced box cutters and broken bottles to corner his attacker—heroes in their own movies. But the jackhammer operator didn't even try to get away. As deflated as the guy he had just let the air out of, he only sank down to the bench normally used by players waiting their turn. He stared at his shoes with that blank expression Mechanic had seen plenty of times on the faces of players who had lost more gambling than they could afford. Before him, others pinned the screaming, sheet-metal worker to the pool table, holding him by the ankles and shoulders so he couldn't make the bleeding worse by pulling out the cue.

The onlookers grew so dense around him that soon Mechanic couldn't see anything but the handle of the pool cue, swaying reed-like above their heads with the rhythm of labored breathing. "Keep it together," someone encouraged. There was a pitiful moan. "Be cool, man!" others advised. "The ambulance is coming!"

As did most of the others in the bar, Mechanic, Designer and Composer sat silently in their booth, taken out of time by the commotion of the fight, then the tenseness of the wait, by the spectacle of first the police arriving—*To Control & Punish*, said the reflective lettering on their jackets—then finally the ambulance. Paramedics in blue coveralls sauntered in carrying toolboxes like the mechanics they were: mechanics who dealt with body fluids instead of radiator leaks even if one of their toolboxes was empty, an ice-chest, as everyone knew, that all the paramedics of IN brought along in case their call for assistance became instead an occasion to harvest an organ. When the police pushed people back to create an aisle for them, Mechanic got a glimpse of the guy, his face ghostly-white against the green of the table. The *Standard Beer* light that hung over the pool table made his naked torso shine—a patient under the lamp of an operating table—now stripped of the clothing the paramedics had cut away. It also illuminated their hands, working first to wrap his punctured body in gauze, then to load it onto a stretcher.

As they took him away, a friend of his called after, "Don't worry about your hardhat, man. I'll bring it to work for you!"

Then it was over.

People milled about, talking about what they'd

— ⓪ —

seen, and what he'd said, and what the other had said back. Someone threw a dart. A chubby drill-press operator in an overly tight tube-top pantomimed the fight for some girlfriends who had arrived after the action. "No way!" they shrieked at her animated explanation.

"I can't believe they would fight over a game," Designer said, her beautiful face flushed. Her lips were even fuller now, an indentation of teeth in her lower lip revealing how tense she had been. Composer described to Designer other fights he had witnessed in this bar, filling in details that seemed self-evident to Mechanic—e.g. "a game can be more than a game"— though judging from Designer's reactions, they were the very things she'd been wondering: the best guide to a foreign culture not being a native, like Mechanic, apparently, but another foreigner, like Composer, even if from him, the cheating hearts, drunken husbands and wasted lives sounded more like the lyrics to a standard blues song.

Gradually the bar returned to normal. Standard bar music began to play again from the standard jukebox. Soon there was a dart game going. And not long after that, another game of Dunk-a-Drunk on the pool table where the man had lain bleeding, the stains he had left on its felt indistinguishable from those left by spilt beer. Composer was back at the point he'd been making when he'd been interrupted by the fight: "...your typical audio composer, though, goes about his or her business listening to the maestro of the slide whistle but never really hearing, and therefore never apprehending how any music that can be bought and sold—even the most anarchist of rock music—is a force in the maintenance of the status quo...."

Listening to Composer explain how "ultimately, what we consider to be music and how we play it determines who and what we are," Mechanic had the gut feeling that he was right; his words did seem to explain why the pool game had meant so much to the loser. But there also seemed to be another thing that Composer was leaving out, something equally important: the fact that the game had meant so much to the two men, Mechanic knew, because their bodies had been in the bargain, the big guy going nuts over the graffiti of the chalk, his body being something so not-to-fuck-with because during the rest of the week all of their bodies were little more than tools that the factories they worked in would slowly consume—like a pencil, or a drill bit—this information also expressed in the lopsided development of the woman in the tube-top, her right arm, but not her left, muscular from operating a drill-press all day.

Two young guys went by with the gimpiness of old geezers, or rather, the gimpiness of carpet layers, Mechanic knew, the premature sponginess in their knees coming from the days they spent on them.

Looking from them to Composer's symmetrical body, and Designer's symmetrical face—and how different their classically proportioned jaws were from the other jaws in the bar, he tried to reconcile what Composer said with what he had seen, what he thought, with how everyone he knew lived: the idea that art could shape its viewer when up until then the only thing that had shaped anyone he had ever known was the world.

"...among composers in the audio spectrum," Composer was saying, "Mallarmé alone understood that the musician who bypasses the senses completely is the musician who creates music *par excellence.*"

The carpet layers started dancing in an area cleared of tables, and were soon joined by the drill-press operator and her friends: women with hairdos of lacquered ringlets so tight their heads could be easily sheathed in the hair nets required of cafeteria workers. As the jukebox mechanically put out the popular hits—love songs that followed their pre-dictable plots—more dancers took to the floor: a line dance of partners whose finger snaps conformed to the arc of a shovel's throw, swirls of skirts echoing the pirouettes of mopping.

"In this they are like viewers who remain fixated on rainbows, mistaking this sliver of visible light for the entire electro-magnetic spectrum, comforting audiences by confirming their assumptions about the good and the natural...." Composer touched Designer's arm for emphasis. She didn't move away. "But tell me, once all music is as popular as door chimes, what will be the point?"

Mechanic wanted to touch her other arm. To tell her how all that Composer said about silence applied equally to machines. Gratefully, he didn't have to: "My friends and I are not so interested in art that pleases by

— ⓪ —

confirming the justice, the naturalness, the nobility, even, of those who, unawares, hold it to be just, and natural, and noble for them to spend their days making cars so they can buy cars to get to jobs where they make cars."

Composer winked at Mechanic, including him.

"B-B-But,..." Mechanic stuttered, struggling for a way to make her see that autos still could be harmonies of beautiful metal that was seen, and beautiful mechanics that remained unseen. Why not?

"We are more interested in X-rays of machines," Composer was saying, "X-rays of music."

"If only there was some way of bringing them together," she answered earnestly.

Yes! Yes! Yes! screamed through Mechanic's mind as his mouth struggled for the words to say it.

Smiling, Composer raised his glass. "To Art."

"And to love!" Mechanic blurted out. He thought Designer gave him a smile. But that may have just been a trick of the light, the bare bulb that hung above their booth sputtering out just at that moment. He licked his lips to continue, to work into the conversation his undying admiration for her, and for what they could do together—Why not?

Just as he found the coordination to speak, though, she said, "Well I like rainbows anyway. They *are* beautiful."

"Yes, but—"

"And if silence is just as important as sound, isn't it just a matter of which one you like better? I mean, what good is art that no one can understand? Or art that no one can stand to look at? Even Aristotle said, That art is best which hides art."

Had Photographer been there, Mechanic knew, he would have launched into her Aristotle like a junk-yard dog into a trespasser.

"Wouldn't it be better," she said, "to take a middle road? To make art everyone can understand and love? Even if it says less?"

As she continued to speak, Mechanic expected Composer to say something in rebuttal to the reasons, or non-reasons, she gave for liking elevator music: that though she didn't know anything about music, she knew what she liked, and what she liked had nothing to do with the reasons they gave for liking. It was beyond liking. Beyond reason, she reasoned, claiming that giving such seduction reason was like diagramming the beauty of a sunset, or a moon rise, the reasons themselves seductive, but in the end seduction and not consummation, not sunset, not moonrise....

Mechanic itched to say something himself, Aristotle obviously not knowing a crankshaft from a carburetor. But Composer only gave a sympathetic nod and answered, "Perhaps." Then he—he who rarely laughed—let out a hearty chuckle, "Yes, perhaps you are completely right. Who can say?" And Mechanic remained silent, the clink of beer bottles the two of them exchanged in front of his face as meaningful as some secret handshake he had been allowed to witness, but not understand.

CHAPTER SEVENTEEN

Did it all come down to cash?

From the vantage of the tollbooth, the highest point in IN not counting Photographer's camera-house, Mechanic could see the OZ skyline glittering like a city molded of diamond dust. The Essence of OZ Building rose highest of all, of course, and he looked onto it longingly, imagining Designer there drawing mythical creatures that would morph into clay models, then real steel, bent and welded by robots in the brown, palm-treed countries from which they emanated, filling the roads of the world, including the one that streamed by him in his tollbooth. $1.00;

— ⓪ —

$1.00; $1.00; $1.00; $1.00; $1.00; $1.00; $1.00;
$1.00; $1.00; $1.00; $1.00; $1.00; $1.00; $1.00;
$1.00; $1.00; $1.00; $1.00; $1.00; $1.00; $1.00;
$1.00; $1.00; $1.00; $1.00; $1.00; $1.00; $1.00;
$1.00; $1.00; $1.00; $1.00; $1.00; $1.00; $1.00;
$1.00; $1.00; $1.00; $1.00; $1.00; $1.00; $1.00;
$1.00; $1.00; $1.00; $1.00; $1.00; $1.00; $1.00;
$1.00; $1.00; $1.00; $1.00; $1.00; $1.00; $1.00;
$1.00; $1.00; $1.00; $1.00; $1.00; $1.00; $1.00;
$1.00; $1.00; $1.00; $1.00; $1.00; $1.00; $1.00;
$1.00; $1.00; $1.00; $1.00; $1.00; $1.00; $1.00;
$1.00; $1.00; $1.00; $1.00; $1.00; $1.00; $1.00;
$1.00; $1.00; $1.00; $1.00; $1.00; $1.00; $1.00;
$1.00; $1.00; $1.00; $1.00; $1.00; $1.00; $1.00;
$1.00; $1.00; $1.00; $1.00; $1.00; $1.00; $1.00;
$1.00; $1.00; $1.00; $1.00; $1.00; $1.00; $1.00;
$1.00; $1.00; $1.00; $1.00; $1.00; $1.00; $1.00;
$1.00; $1.00; $1.00; $1.00; $1.00; $1.00; $1.00;
$1.00; $1.00; $1.00; $1.00; $1.00; $1.00; $1.00;
$1.00; $1.00; $1.00; $1.00; $1.00; $1.00; $1.00;
$1.00; $1.00; $1.00; $1.00; $1.00; $1.00; $1.00;
$1.00; $1.00; $1.00; $1.00; $1.00; $1.00; $1.00;
$1.00; $1.00; $1.00; $1.00; $1.00; $1.00; $1.00;
$1.00; $1.00; $1.00; $1.00; $1.00; $1.00; $1.00;
$1.00; $1.00; $1.00; $1.00; $1.00; $1.00; $1.00;
$1.00; $1.00; $1.00; $1.00; $1.00; $1.00; $1.00;
$1.00; $1.00; $1.00; $1.00; $1.00; $1.00; $1.00;
$1.00; $1.00; $1.00; $1.00; $1.00; $1.00; $1.00;
$1.00; $1.00; $1.00; $1.00; $1.00; $1.00; $1.00;
$1.00; $1.00; $1.00; $1.00; $1.00; $1.00; $1.00;
$1.00; $1.00; $1.00; $1.00; $1.00; $1.00; $1.00:

— ⓪ —

$1.00; $1.00; $1.00; $1.00; $1.00; $1.00; $1.00;
$1.00; $1.00; $1.00; $1.00; $1.00; $1.00; $1.00;
$1.00; $1.00; $1.00; $1.00; $1.00; $1.00; $1.00;
$1.00; $1.00; $1.00; $1.00; $1.00; $1.00; $1.00;
$1.00; $1.00; $1.00; $1.00; $1.00; $1.00; $1.00;
$1.00; $1.00; $1.00; $1.00; $1.00; $1.00; $1.00;
$1.00; $1.00; $1.00; $1.00; $1.00; $1.00; $1.00;
$1.00; $1.00; $1.00; $1.00; $1.00; $1.00; $1.00;
$1.00; $1.00; $1.00; $1.00; $1.00; $1.00; $1.00;
$1.00; $1.00; $1.00; $1.00; $1.00; $1.00; $1.00;
$1.00; $1.00; $1.00; $1.00; $1.00; $1.00; $1.00;
$1.00; $1.00; $1.00; $1.00; $1.00; $1.00; $1.00;
$1.00; $1.00; $1.00; $1.00; $1.00; $1.00; $1.00;
$1.00; $1.00; $1.00; $1.00; $1.00; $1.00; $1.00;
$1.00; $1.00; $1.00; $1.00; $1.00; $1.00; $1.00;
$1.00; $1.00; $1.00; $1.00; $1.00; $1.00; $1.00;
$1.00; $1.00; $1.00; $1.00; $1.00; $1.00; $1.00;
$1.00; $1.00; $1.00; $1.00; $1.00; $1.00; $1.00;
$1.00; $1.00; $1.00; $1.00; $1.00; $1.00; $1.00;
$1.00; $1.00; $1.00; $1.00; $1.00; $1.00; $1.00;
$1.00; $1.00; $1.00; $1.00; $1.00; $1.00; $1.00;
$1.00; $1.00; $1.00; $1.00; $1.00; $1.00; $1.00;
$1.00; $1.00; $1.00; $1.00; $1.00; $1.00; $1.00;
$1.00; $1.00; $1.00; $1.00; $1.00; $1.00; $1.00;
$1.00; $1.00; $1.00; $1.00; $1.00; $1.00; $1.00;
$1.00; $1.00; $1.00; $1.00; $1.00; $1.00; $1.00;
$1.00; $1.00; $1.00; $1.00; $1.00; $1.00; $1.00;
$1.00; $1.00; $1.00; $1.00; $1.00; $1.00; $1.00;
$1.00; $1.00; $1.00; $1.00; $1.00; $1.00; $1.00;
$1.00; $1.00; $1.00; $1.00; $1.00; $1.00; $1.00;

— 0 —

$1.00; $1.00; $1.00; $1.00; $1.00; $1.00; $1.00;
$1.00; $1.00; $1.00; $1.00; $1.00; $1.00; $1.00;
$1.00; $1.00; $1.00; $1.00; $1.00; $1.00; $1.00;
$1.00; $1.00; $1.00; $1.00; $1.00; $1.00; $1.00;
$1.00; $1.00; $1.00; $1.00; $1.00; $1.00; $1.00;
$1.00; $1.00; $1.00; $1.00; $1.00; $1.00; $1.00;
$1.00; $1.00; $1.00; $1.00; $1.00; $1.00; $1.00;
$1.00; $1.00; $1.00; $1.00; $1.00; $1.00; $1.00;
$1.00; $1.00; $1.00; $1.00; $1.00; $1.00; $1.00;
$1.00; $1.00; $1.00; $1.00; $1.00; $1.00; $1.00;
$1.00; $1.00; $1.00; $1.00; $1.00; $1.00; $1.00;
$1.00; $1.00; $1.00; $1.00; $1.00; $1.00; $1.00;
$1.00; $1.00; $1.00; $1.00; $1.00; $1.00; $1.00;
$1.00; $1.00; $1.00; $1.00; $1.00; $1.00; $1.00;
$1.00; $1.00; $1.00; $1.00; $1.00; $1.00; $1.00;
$1.00; $1.00; $1.00; $1.00; $1.00; $1.00; $1.00;
$1.00; $1.00; $1.00; $1.00; $1.00; $1.00; $1.00;
$1.00; $1.00; $1.00; $1.00; $1.00; $1.00; $1.00;
$1.00; $1.00; $1.00; $1.00; $1.00; $1.00; $1.00;
$1.00; $1.00; $1.00; $1.00; $1.00; $1.00; $1.00;
$1.00; $1.00; $1.00; $1.00; $1.00; $1.00; $1.00;
$1.00; $1.00; $1.00; $1.00; $1.00; $1.00; $1.00;
$1.00; $1.00; $1.00; $1.00; $1.00; $1.00; $1.00;
$1.00; $1.00; $1.00; $1.00; $1.00; $1.00; $1.00;
$1.00; $1.00; $1.00; $1.00; $1.00; $1.00; $1.00;
$1.00; $1.00; $1.00; $1.00; $1.00; $1.00; $1.00;
$1.00; $1.00; $1.00; $1.00; $1.00; $1.00; $1.00;
$1.00; $1.00; $1.00; $1.00; $1.00; $1.00; $1.00;
$1.00; $1.00; $1.00; $1.00; $1.00; $1.00; $1.00;
$1.00; $1.00; $1.00; $1.00; $1.00; $1.00; $1.00:

— ⓪ —

$1.00; $1.00; $1.00; $1.00; $1.00; $1.00; $1.00;
$1.00; $1.00; $1.00; $1.00; $1.00; $1.00; $1.00;
$1.00; $1.00; $1.00; $1.00; $1.00; $1.00; $1.00;
$1.00; $1.00; $1.00; $1.00; $1.00; $1.00; $1.00;
$1.00; $1.00; $1.00; $1.00; $1.00; $1.00; $1.00;
$1.00; $1.00; $1.00; $1.00; $1.00; $1.00; $1.00;
$1.00; $1.00; $1.00; $1.00; $1.00; $1.00; $1.00;
$1.00; $1.00; $1.00; $1.00; $1.00; $1.00; $1.00;
$1.00; $1.00; $1.00; $1.00; $1.00; $1.00; $1.00;
$1.00; $1.00; $1.00; $1.00; $1.00; $1.00; $1.00;
$1.00; $1.00; $1.00; $1.00; $1.00; $1.00; $1.00;
$1.00; $1.00; $1.00; $1.00; $1.00; $1.00; $1.00;
$1.00; $1.00; $1.00; $1.00; $1.00; $1.00; $1.00;
$1.00; $1.00; $1.00; $1.00; $1.00; $1.00; $1.00;
$1.00; $1.00; $1.00; $1.00; $1.00; $1.00; $1.00;
$1.00; $1.00; $1.00; $1.00; $1.00; $1.00; $1.00;
$1.00; $1.00; $1.00; $1.00; $1.00; $1.00; $1.00;
$1.00; $1.00; $1.00; $1.00; $1.00; $1.00; $1.00;
$1.00; $1.00; $1.00; $1.00; $1.00; $1.00; $1.00;
$1.00; $1.00; $1.00; $1.00; $1.00; $1.00; $1.00;
$1.00; $1.00; $1.00; $1.00; $1.00; $1.00; $1.00;
$1.00; $1.00; $1.00; $1.00; $1.00; $1.00; $1.00;
$1.00; $1.00; $1.00; $1.00; $1.00; $1.00; $1.00;
$1.00; $1.00; $1.00; $1.00; $1.00; $1.00; $1.00;
$1.00; $1.00; $1.00; $1.00; $1.00; $1.00; $1.00;
$1.00; $1.00; $1.00; $1.00; $1.00; $1.00; $1.00;
$1.00; $1.00; $1.00; $1.00; $1.00; $1.00; $1.00;
$1.00; $1.00; $1.00; $1.00; $1.00; $1.00; $1.00;
$1.00; $1.00; $1.00; $1.00; $1.00; $1.00; $1.00;
$1.00; $1.00; $1.00; $1.00; $1.00; $1.00; $1.00;
$1.00; $1.00; $1.00; $1.00; $1.00; $1.00; $1.00:

— ① —

$1.00; $1.00; $1.00; $1.00; $1.00; $1.00; $1.00;
$1.00; $1.00; $1.00; $1.00; $1.00; $1.00; $1.00;
$1.00; $1.00; $1.00; $1.00; $1.00; $1.00; $1.00;
$1.00; $1.00; $1.00; $1.00; $1.00; $1.00; $1.00;
$1.00; $1.00; $1.00; $1.00; $1.00; $1.00; $1.00;
$1.00; $1.00; $1.00; $1.00; $1.00; $1.00; $1.00;
$1.00; $1.00; $1.00; $1.00; $1.00; $1.00; $1.00;
$1.00; $1.00; $1.00; $1.00; $1.00; $1.00; $1.00;
$1.00; $1.00; $1.00; $1.00; $1.00; $1.00; $1.00;
$1.00; $1.00; $1.00; $1.00; $1.00; $1.00; $1.00;
$1.00; $1.00; $1.00; $1.00; $1.00; $1.00; $1.00;
$1.00; $1.00; $1.00; $1.00; $1.00; $1.00; $1.00;
$1.00; $1.00; $1.00; $1.00; $1.00; $1.00; $1.00;
$1.00; $1.00; $1.00; $1.00; $1.00; $1.00; $1.00;
$1.00; $1.00; $1.00; $1.00; $1.00; $1.00; $1.00;
$1.00; $1.00; $1.00; $1.00; $1.00; $1.00; $1.00;
$1.00; $1.00; $1.00; $1.00; $1.00; $1.00; $1.00;
$1.00; $1.00; $1.00; $1.00; $1.00; $1.00; $1.00;
$1.00; $1.00; $1.00; $1.00; $1.00; $1.00; $1.00;
$1.00; $1.00; $1.00; $1.00; $1.00; $1.00; $1.00;
$1.00; $1.00; $1.00; $1.00; $1.00; $1.00; $1.00;
$1.00; $1.00; $1.00; $1.00; $1.00; $1.00; $1.00;
$1.00; $1.00; $1.00; $1.00; $1.00; $1.00; $1.00;
$1.00; $1.00; $1.00; $1.00; $1.00; $1.00; $1.00;
$1.00; $1.00; $1.00; $1.00; $1.00; $1.00; $1.00;
$1.00; $1.00; $1.00; $1.00; $1.00; $1.00; $1.00;
$1.00; $1.00; $1.00; $1.00; $1.00; $1.00; $1.00;
$1.00; $1.00; $1.00; $1.00; $1.00; $1.00; $1.00;
$1.00; $1.00; $1.00; $1.00; $1.00; $1.00; $1.00;
$1.00; $1.00; $1.00; $1.00; $1.00; $1.00; $1.00;

— ⓪ —

$1.00; \quad $1.00; \quad $1.00; \quad $1.00; \quad $1.00; \quad $1.00; \quad $1.00;
$1.00; \quad $1.00; \quad $1.00; \quad $1.00; \quad $1.00; \quad $1.00; \quad $1.00;
$1.00; \quad $1.00; \quad $1.00; \quad $1.00; \quad $1.00; \quad $1.00; \quad $1.00;
$1.00; \quad $1.00; \quad $1.00; \quad $1.00; \quad $1.00; \quad $1.00; \quad $1.00;
$1.00; \quad $1.00; \quad $1.00; \quad $1.00; \quad $1.00; \quad $1.00; \quad $1.00;
$1.00; \quad $1.00; \quad $1.00; \quad $1.00; \quad $1.00; \quad $1.00; \quad $1.00;
$1.00; \quad $1.00; \quad $1.00; \quad $1.00; \quad $1.00; \quad $1.00; \quad $1.00;
$1.00; \quad $1.00; \quad $1.00; \quad $1.00; \quad $1.00; \quad $1.00; \quad $1.00;
$1.00; \quad $1.00; \quad $1.00; \quad $1.00; \quad $1.00; \quad $1.00; \quad $1.00;
$1.00; \quad $1.00; \quad $1.00; \quad $1.00; \quad $1.00; \quad $1.00; \quad $1.00;
$1.00; \quad $1.00; \quad $1.00; \quad $1.00; \quad $1.00; \quad $1.00; \quad $1.00;
$1.00; \quad $1.00; \quad $1.00; \quad $1.00; \quad $1.00; \quad $1.00; \quad $1.00;
$1.00; \quad $1.00; \quad $1.00; \quad $1.00; \quad $1.00; \quad $1.00; \quad $1.00;
$1.00; \quad $1.00; \quad $1.00; \quad $1.00; \quad $1.00; \quad $1.00; \quad $1.00;
$1.00; \quad $1.00; \quad $1.00; \quad $1.00; \quad $1.00; \quad $1.00; \quad $1.00;
$1.00; \quad $1.00; \quad $1.00; \quad $1.00; \quad $1.00; \quad $1.00; \quad $1.00;
$1.00; \quad $1.00; \quad $1.00; \quad $1.00; \quad $1.00; \quad $1.00; \quad $1.00;
$1.00; \quad $1.00; \quad $1.00; \quad $1.00; \quad $1.00; \quad $1.00; \quad $1.00;
$1.00; \quad $1.00; \quad $1.00; \quad $1.00; \quad $1.00; \quad $1.00; \quad $1.00;
$1.00; \quad $1.00; \quad $1.00; \quad $1.00; \quad $1.00; \quad $1.00; \quad $1.00;
$1.00; \quad $1.00; \quad $1.00; \quad $1.00; \quad $1.00; \quad $1.00; \quad $1.00;
$1.00; \quad $1.00; \quad $1.00; \quad $1.00; \quad $1.00; \quad $1.00; \quad $1.00;
$1.00; \quad $1.00; \quad $1.00; \quad $1.00; \quad $1.00; \quad $1.00; \quad $1.00;
$1.00; \quad $1.00; \quad $1.00; \quad $1.00; \quad $1.00; \quad $1.00; \quad $1.00;
$1.00; \quad $1.00; \quad $1.00; \quad $1.00; \quad $1.00; \quad $1.00; \quad $1.00;
$1.00; \quad $1.00; \quad $1.00; \quad $1.00; \quad $1.00; \quad $1.00; \quad $1.00;
$1.00; \quad $1.00; \quad $1.00; \quad $1.00; \quad $1.00; \quad $1.00; \quad $1.00;
$1.00; $1.00; $1.00; $1.00; $1.00; $1.00....

Before coming to the tollbooth, he had no idea of the number of people who saw Designer's art, and

— ① —

were carried along by her art, and were comforted by her art. But now he knew: everyone. Or everyone who mattered. Or rather everyone with money, which seemed to be the same as everyone who mattered. Eight hours a day he took a dollar from a steady procession of them, and saw up-close how her art shaped this human comedy with harried businesswomen looking through the scrolling multi-colored ticker-tapes projected on their windshields so that they could follow stock reports without taking their eyes off the road; or the drowsy, gently guided into the narrow lane of his booth by technology developed for the nose cones of missiles; or lovers nestled within velvet clouds that had once been a dream in Designer's mind, while mobsters didn't have to lift a pinkie-ringed finger to yell into cell phones that she, in her infinite wisdom, had wisely drawn into their dashboards. When the power window of one car automatically lowered itself so that its driver could pay his toll, Bedouin flute music and the scent of jasmine rolled out from his private harem that was a mosh pit to the next driver, hard-pounding techno-trance socking out from her pugilistic-sound system. These and a thousand other drivers passed by his booth, the utter joy they took from her art—if it wasn't as invisible to them as their very breath—telling him how utterly uninterested they would be in the stuff of his art. Some didn't even bother to hide the disgust they felt toward him for breaking the dream of driving as he did being there as he was to take their toll.

— ⓪ —

$1.00 $1.00

$1.00

$1.00

Hand out, dollar in, hand out, dollar in…. The mechanical repetitiveness of extending a hand, retracting a dollar, then extending a hand became a kind of mantra to him, lulling him to thought. He had a lot to think about. Soon, he would finally finish the hydraulic bouquet he'd been constructing for Designer, and the thought of the moment when he would actually give it to her filled him with dread. She was so big—such an influential artist while he was?— What?

$1.00; $1.00; $1.00; $1.00….

A fool for thinking that what she did and what he did could ever be married? $1.00; $1.00; $1.00; $1.00; $1.00; $1.00; $1.00; $1.00; $1.00; $1.00….

Photographer and Composer might say it didn't matter, especially Photographer. But deep down, with the world voting in dollars, and voting for her and her invisible cars, only a true fool would not have doubts.

$1.00

$1.00

$1.00

$1.00

$1.00….

A horrid thought suddenly brought him up by the short hairs: What if a person could only see what he had seen by crawling under a car to see it?

— ⓪ —

As if summoned by fate to illustrate what he was thinking, he spotted a figure far below, at the base of the hill, laboring to push a bicycle up its steep grade.

What if crawling through sludge, exhaling to collapse your chest so that you could squeeze into the narrow space afforded by a jack was the only way to see it? he thought, watching her. He could tell that it was definitely a her, pushing her bike up a hill that made walking easier than pedalling. Cars whizzed past, honking their horns as angrily at her as they honked at him and his car.

Maybe if Designer found a way to bring what he saw out into the light for everyone, they would see something, but it wouldn't be It. The possibility made him shudder.

Then he held his breath. As the bicyclist neared, he could see that it was Poet (Sculptor).

He could also see why she was pushing her bicycle. Unlike modern OZ bikes with their featherweight construction and delicate derailers that made pedalling uphill easy, her bike seemed to have been designed by a boiler company. Its brown, primer-colored frame had the rigidity and heaviness of the bridge's girders and made easing it into the line of cars waiting to pay their toll awkward for her.

$1.00 $1.00 $1.00

She moved, in the line, a little closer.

Perspiration painted big oval stains on the underarms of her work shirt, its sleeves rolled up and revealing sinewy forearms. She had used duct tape to make a bicycle cuff on one leg of her standard, factory-uniform trousers.

— ⓪ —

$1.00 $1.00

       $1.00

Then she was close enough for him to see strands of hair matted on her forehead, brush marks in the paint of her bicycle, her bicycle obviously having been painted by hand with leftover house paint.

"Hello," he said, as she came up to his booth.

She smiled, nodded her hello back, breathing hard to catch her breath, her face flushed, her flat chest huffing. She was radiant from the exertion. He hadn't noticed how beautiful she was till the work of climbing the hill pointed it out.

"One dollar, please," he said. She dug around in the mouth of a homemade metal purse that looked like a fish; its scales were overlapping, flattened bottle caps.

One, two, three, four....

Watching her count out pennies, reading her lips as she did so, he took pleasure in how easy it was to be with her here in the narrow lane of the tollbooth. How easy it was to talk to her, to understand her, the constraints of the tollbooth transaction keeping their conversation from bleeding all over into topics with no bounds, or the messy groping about that troubled Mechanic in most other conversations where you could never really tell what was truly being said, or what the other person really wanted.

...forty-four, forty-five, forty-six, forty-seven, forty-eight, forty-nine, fifty. She paused, looking up to him, and he understood that she wanted him to take the first half of the toll. When he did, their hands touched.

...fifty-one, fifty-two, fifty-three....

— ⓪ —

If only all of life could be so clear! As she contin-ued to count, he wracked his brain for a way to stretch the moment. What *did* men and women talk about, anyway!

...seventy-nine, eighty, eighty-one....

Politics! "I—I—I'm sorry about the vote," he stam-mered.

The dismissive shrug he received in reply froze his heart. Leading up to the referendum on limiting bill-board space, the campaign had grown more intense with each side pushing the envelope of billboarding while language did what language always does, and some of the anti-billboard-istas began to appreciate writing on pages that were twenty-feet high. To these poor fallible men and women who had never had an audience other than themselves, Photographer had explained, the thousands of motorists who streamed by and read their words—their words!—was intoxicating beyond bearability. In secret, they had begun to work against the limitation of billboards. A form of censor-ship. Some of the pro-billboard-ists, on the other hand, began to loath the increasing difficulty they had in cut-ting through the "poetic static," as they called it, with the poetry of their products. Secretly, they began to work to limit the number of billboards. That is, some anti became defacto-pro and some pro became defacto-anti-billboarders, and in the end voters decided by ref-erendum to freeze the number of billboards at their new, elevated level, which half of the pro-billboarders took as defeat, and half of the anti-billboarders took as defeat, and half of the pro-billboarders took as victory, and half of the anti-billboarders took as victory, though it was impossible to tell which half was which.

Had he insulted her? "I mean— I'm glad!" he blurted. Why had he stepped outside of the easy give-and-take of the tollbooth!

Again she only shrugged, exactly as before, and finished counting out pennies from her fish purse.

"I mean— I mean, I'd like to see some of your poetry one day."

She paused, giving him a wry?—or maybe it was a condescending smile.

"I mean your sculpture?"

Her head cocked like a dog hearing an odd squeal.

"I mean your dirt."

She placed the second fifty coins in his hand. Their hands touched again, hers lingering this time. Or was it just his imagination?—the moment seemed to stop during which every detail was so vivid it made him ache: her chewed fingernails, the sweet stink of her sweat, the whiteness of the balls of her knuckles made even more pure by the dirt in their creases that he knew from the engine grime under his own finger-nails would never come clean. Not so long as she kept dirt as her medium....

The driver of the next car honked impatiently.

Then her sinewy hands were taking up the grips of her handlebars. But she nodded as she rotated a pedal into position, a serene expression coming over her face to let him know that someday she'd show him some.

"Well goodbye," he said.

She smiled back, then pushed off, as happily as if

— ⓪ —

the vote had never happened. A moment later he saw her legs kick out from each side of her bike as she allowed the gravity of the hill to speed her along, coasting, the wind whipping her shirttail as the bicycle picked up speed, her arms suddenly shooting up into a victory V as well....

How did she do it? he wondered. How did she manage to float above it all? No more concerned by votes, or cash, or even whether people walked all over the dirt of the earth, not giving a shit whether or not it was her art?

For a long time afterwards, he replayed in his mind that vision of her coasting downhill, picking up speed, the wind whipping the tails of her work shirt as he tried to puzzle out her secret and why, even if he could, it wouldn't work for him.

It wasn't that Mechanic was unsympathetic to the claim made by Poet (Sculptor)'s silence—that the gesture of making dirt your medium was enough. He himself had gone on for the longest time without telling anyone what he had seen, and he might have continued to fix cars in the traditional sense indefinitely had he not begun to fear that Artistic Truths unshared had a name: hallucinations.

$1.00 $1.00 $1.00 $1.00
$1.00 $1.00

It was just that it was hard to believe that the actual medium of all art was dirt. Or cash. Or that fashion was the most honest solution, as Designer maintained—dirt and cash being the Yin to the other's Yang with sales as the only True artistic review, every other

— ⓪ —

judgment being a matter of simple preference, a gas gauge on half empty/ half full, toe-mae-toe/ toe-maa-toe, you like standard vanilla/ I like piña colada, so what's all the fuss about? But if that were so, then the swings between the seen and the unseen that so exercised Photographer—the swings between the Greeks and their sculptures of beautiful bodies, to the Medieval art of the unseen spirit that could start him frothing at the mouth—were of no more consequence than the changes in the width of neckties or the styles of hem lengths.

He didn't know a lot about the history of art. But he did know a little about the history of autos, or at least the Standard Autos that were once manufactured in IN, the first of which was a plow.

Turning from OZ, he looked onto the browness of IN, flat as mud except for the few decaying turn-of-the-century mansions. One of them, the house of an industrialist from the days when autos were assembled by human hands, had been restored and turned into a museum and home of the IN Historical Society and Gun Enthusiasts Club.

$1.00

$1.00 $1.00 $1.00....

As Mechanic mechanically took in the bills, he began to wander the displays of the museum in his mind, walking along with Designer, and Composer, and Photographer and Poet (Sculptor), taking advantage of the one perk that came with most of the jobs in IN: the fact that as his body continued to do its work, his mind could leave, entering what passed in IN for Virtual Reality. The first exhibit they approached was of a farm plow which, as a plaque explained, had been manufactured by the Blacksmith who founded the Standard Plow and Feed Co. back in the days when the last of the Indian trading paths were becoming dirt roads. Poet (Sculptor) ran ahead of the group, admiring the homey simplicity of a replica of the rough log cabin where the Blacksmith/Founder was shown forging the first plow. For a generation the company did well, Composer read to the group from the plaque. But as IN grew and others began to make Improved Standard Plows, then the wheelbarrows, wagons and carriages that Blacksmith & Sons had begun to produce, the company faltered and would have gone under if it hadn't been saved by the outbreak of the Civil War that allowed them to beat plow blades into swords and bayonets which they sold to both sides at a very high profit. The next war, WWI, was even better for business, they learned, moving on to a motorized diorama: sections of plaster-of-Paris farmland and painted scenery rotated to the underside of the table that the diorama was built on while slag pits and factories that had been on the underside of the table rotated up to take their place in the growth of IN. Connected by rail as never before to sources of coal, steel and lumber, the company was able to capitalize on a single design, the Standard Design, that allowed them to output a carriage every five hours, modifying each during production to be either a horse-drawn buggy for Sunday drives or a wheeled cannon mount. They also made their first horseless carriage: a motorized vehicle which could be fitted with a Gatling gun for military use, but was in fact first used to break up a strike by workers at a factory that supplied the rivets in its frame.

The expansion that had been fueled by the war allowed the company—now known as The Standard Automobile & Armament Factory—to again survive the peace, this time by making automobiles: black carriages with gasoline engines that had to be started with a crank. It was during this period that the mansion had been built, the great-great grandsons of the original Blacksmith having grown so very rich and powerful that once a President even spent the night in their mansion. A third shift had been added and production ran night and day. By this time the shifts of SAAF were a kind of nature to the people of IN, the factory whistle marking the rising and setting of their sons who grew up to become their fathers on its assembly lines though Photographer pointed out that this history was not so evident in the history of IN that was written in the sheets of metal they forged, a history that ran from the black carriages to the sedans with running boards for gangsters to stand on, to the amphibious troop carriers and rocket launchers of WWII, then the tail fins and flamboyant hood ornaments when times were good, which fell away as times grew lean and the expected WWIII remained forever just beyond the horizon.

The last car the company ever made was a single prototype built for a World's Fair: a Futuristic Car of the
Future from a future that, of course, never came.

The group stood in reverent silence, their funhouse
reflections dim in the tarnished titanium of this last
car, shaped like a torpedo with high rocket fins. In the
hush of the museum, the memento mori moved
Mechanic to thoughts of his own dead parents, and
how blueprints for this still-born future must have
been created at about the same time that his father,
who had never intended to be a mechanic, had opened
his garage. Living under a bridge as Mechanic's father
and mother did, whenever someone's car broke down it
would coast downhill and end up at their door. Usually
owners of the broken cars simply asked to use the
phone. Sometimes they would ask his father to have a
look-see at the engine. Eventually, the increasing business brought on by the ever-more severe cost-cutting
measures at the plant forced him to put up a hand-
lettered sign listing fees for various repairs. He never
returned from his next layoff, having metamorphosed
during it into a full-time mechanic.

Following the group into the art gallery of the
museum, Mechanic had all of this in mind, taking in
the succession of company calendars that hung there
depicting the evolution of the factory with its ever-
more modern train loads of coal and trees at one end,
acres of completed cars at the other, plumes of PROS-
PERITY issuing from each of the factory's many
smokestacks. One photo showed a heraldic shield
fashioned from the oranges, greens and browns of

autumn— Trees in autumn, Mechanic and the others realized, once they were close enough to see that the heraldic shield was actually an aerial view of a forest that had been cleared in such a way so that the trees left standing would form a corporate logo the size of a small fiefdom. There were other portraits of inheritance: an unbroken lineage from the painting of a long-bearded founding father, all the way up to a studio photo of a smiling, great-great-great CEO-grandson, posing with his movie-star wife as if the more money earned, the more attractive the people making it became. There was no other art. And looking at this art history, Mechanic saw how if his parents had not lived under a bridge, neither he nor his father would have been a mechanic. Had his parents lived under a bridge that crossed a river of water instead of a river of chemicals that sometimes caught fire, he might have grown up a fisherman. And it astounded him to think that something so central to his being could be so arbitrary— Could it be the same for whole cities? Whole nations?

Tours through the Historical Society and Gun Club always ended on the top floor of the mansion, the ballroom. There, he, Composer, Poet (Sculptor), Photographer, Designer and the other visitors were invited to imagine (and mourn the passing of) the fabulous parties that were once held there, the ballroom situated so that the picture window at one end looked out onto the future that would become OZ, while the picture window at the opposite end had been aligned to give a clear view of the factory's main smokestack, rising like an brick phallus from the abandoned work-houses, slag heaps and assembly lines below, "A still-living monument," the guide said, "to the family's wealth, power, birthright, and legacy."

$1.00; $1.00; $1.00; $1.00; $1.00....

If he ever rubbed a headlamp, Mechanic thought, and a genie appeared to grant him three wishes, he would ask of the genie the answer to three questions:

Question 1: Life.

Question 2: Death.

Question 3: Stuff.

Question 3: Stuff.

Question 3: Stuff.

CHAPTER EIGHTEEN

After that night in the bar, Designer thought about all Composer had said. Thought a lot about commerce being a language, as he had said. And whether or not all things could be said in every language, as he denied. She thought a lot about whether the language she used shaped what she said, but mostly she fretted about the difference between what it made her and what he said was Art.

She sat in the living room of her condo, looking at furnishings she had picked, she thought, to be an expression of her self, but now seeing how she could be an extension of them, living within a spread from *Condo Beautiful* or some other high-end magazine devoted to the art of tasteful living. How could those magazines—products themselves—not have modeled her space, and therefore her vision, and therefore her thoughts, and therefore her work, and therefore herself? Her chrome love-seat came from a celebrity shoot in *Celebrity Living*, vases that looked like a single sheet of folded snow came from another magazine, as did candle holders that could have been huge chrome tears, her white-leather sofa, white rug and all the rest of her furnishings all eloquently saying the same thing: money. As composer said they would.

She'd even picked out her white dog to match the rug, she remembered as it trotted into the room. It sat before her and looked up as if to ask, Could putting something in her condo that didn't come from a magazine make a difference?

She sat up straight.

The dog's ears cocked, eyes on her.

Something that couldn't be bought from a magazine, or even a catalog? Would breaking up the monolithic style of her decor crack open a new way of seeing? In the instant that the rut she'd been in materialized before her, she was also sure that she'd stumbled upon a way out.

But what could she possibly get that didn't come from a store *and* that could shake up her work?

She snapped her fingers when it came to her: Art—as Composer had said all along.

The next day after work, she swung by the gallery district of OZ, and stepping into the first white-walled, hardwood-floored space, she tingled with expectation. A gallery, she saw, was far different from a store. The ratio of merch to clerks was just the opposite of a store, with there being very few works of art on the bare walls, and lots of clerks, impeccably groomed in sleek black dresses, and paid, apparently, to do nothing more than lounge around, filling the gallery with their hip hairstyles and lean beauty.

The art didn't have any prices. Or rather, everything had a price. It was just that determining the price of something as unique and ephemeral as art could only be a matter of discussion—not looking at a tag—in a language with a way of speaking all its own. In order to buy a work of art as opposed to a product, she learned, the gallery owner (shop keeper) and the collector (shopper) would talk about everything but the price—the saturated colors in the clown's outfit, for example, or the fine modeling that the artist employed in rendering the tear beneath his eye—how real it looked!—until an agreed-upon price would emerge from the fog of language like a dove that a magician might produce from a pile of scarves.

Not knowing anything about Art other than that she would know it when she saw it, she went from gallery to gallery, viewing their wares until suddenly there it was— A huge square canvas, painted blue with a yellow swirl. The swirl seemed to spiral down into the center of the painting like the eye of a hurricane seen from above, its intense yellow arms feathering out into the powder-blue background. Even though the chalky, Easter-egg colors formed a pleasing composition, she could tell this abstract painting was a work of Art and not just a pretty picture, as Composer might say, because try as she might, she couldn't understand it. And in the end, she didn't really even care to look at it that much.

Sure enough, the minute she got it home, it began to complicate her life. Here in her condo, the painting was much larger than it had appeared in the open space of the gallery. Her dog growled at it. She took down the designer mirror she'd had hanging over the fireplace, and put the painting up in its place. Seeing it from the couch, her dog cowering in her lap, the painting so big and dominating that she felt it was looking down its nose at her and her apartment as if they were unworthy of its presence. She put the mirror back up and hung the painting on the opposite wall, but trapped between the painting and its mirror image, the concentric swirl gave her a spinning sensation, the swirl itself seeming to rotate like the pinwheels used by hypnotists to gain control of a person's mind until she could think of nothing else.

The only place to hang the painting in the bathroom was across from the toilet, but the blue water, the yellow swirl seemed like a potty joke here. In her bedroom, while laying on her bed and looking at the painting framed by the V of her open legs, it reminded her too much of a bull's-eye, so she moved it back to its original place above the mantel.

Being a designer, she soon found a way to make the Art seem less like a dominating sneer, though. She placed some asymmetrical flowers beside it on the mantel—in a vase that matched, and therefore drew the eye from the blue background of the painting. In *Elegant Living Illustrated*, she found a pair of pillows for sale that had beadwork in a color and pattern that matched the painting exactly and put these on the couch. A lamp from *Elegant Interiors* had the squarish proportions of the painting as did the end table from *Modern Living* that she placed it upon. As time passed and she grew accustomed to the painting and the other new merch in her condo, she found it harder and harder to say which was product and which art. And one day, trying to remember why she had gone out and paid so much for the painting, she clapped her hands together and laughed to realize that she'd found a real answer to the question that had sent her out on her quest. And she had the painting to thank.

CHAPTER NINETEEN

That night, Mechanic arced the last weld on the bouquet he was making for Designer. He tilted his helmet up to admire his handiwork, licked his lips, then hit the START button. The enormous orchid of metal groaned; the fenders he had hammered into petal shapes shrieked the scream of sheet-metal being separated by the Jaws of Life as they opened in bloom: the hundreds of side-view mirrors that he had salvaged from smashed-up cars of Her design rose pistil-like from its center....

Waiting to be pollinated....

Excitedly, he closed up his garage, then set off to find Composer so he could add the last missing bit: a piece of music that would play from the orchid and speak of the difference Composer had been so eloquent about that night in the tavern, a piece of music, or silence, so eloquent that Designer would know that how things worked was at least as important as how they looked—if they didn't, in fact, comprise a whole, a single beat, an infinite slide-whistle.

He found Composer alone in his hole. Before he could even get the request out, though, Composer said, "She wants me to compose a piece of music for her."

"Who?" Mechanic asked happily. The moment he asked, though, he saw the grim expression on Composer's face and held his breath, dreading but unable to believe what he knew would be the answer.

"Designer," Composer said. Mechanic felt his body become a crash-test dummy, the wooden heart inside of that dummy another dummy with a dummy's heart and all of them broken against a wall. By the time his body had warmed enough for him to resume breathing, Composer was saying, "...and wants me to compose a piece of music that can be whistled by the grill of the automobile she is now designing."

"A piece of?— Of *audio* music?" Mechanic finally managed to get out.

Composer nodded. "There's more. She's convinced her company to create a Department of Automotive Musik Engineering. They want me to become its Maestro and Chief Engineer."

Mechanic wanted to think this was a joke. It was the only way his mind could register the barely recognizable quacking he was hearing. "Then you?— And HER?— Would work together?"

Composer looked away. The two of them were silent a long time, feeling the blackness of the hole deepen.

— ⓪ —

"And you?" Mechanic asked. "What do you think?"

Whereas once Composer would have answered with a sneer at what *they* considered music to be, now he shrugged. "Overnight I would have a world-wide audience," he said. Overnight I would be paid. And paid well for my work."

"But it would be your work, not your music," Mechanic said. Composer again fell into the silence of the justly-accused, and the stillness allowed the ghosts of hundreds of smoky conversations to drift up around them. As from a far away place Mechanic heard a ghostly *Yankee Doodle*—with Composer's voice at its edge gushing over the utter genius of the Mallarmé arrangement with its last phrase containing the entire melody the way a Russian nesting doll contains a smaller duplicate of itself. *"Halve the note and double the beat and place the song within itselffff,"* Composer's specter sang to the tune, *"And sing a song about itself that's caught up in its singgggg-inggggg...."*

That song saved my soul, he'd always said, claiming that it taught him the truth about all music. And life: that it was only by paying the strictest attention to music, and not by pandering to the masses, that a musician could discover a subject grander than music. Remembering his claim now, Mechanic spat back at him, "Then Le Petomane was just a story? A fairy tale, meant to amuse drinking buddies?" Again Composer looked away, cut to the quick this time, and for a moment, Mechanic regretted throwing back in his face the French vaudeville performer who was able to fart at will and with such force that he would begin his act by blowing out the candles on a birthday cake. Through the course of his performances, Composer would always say whenever the subject of artists prostituting their work came up, Le Petomane would spread and flex his buttocks to play musical scales, folk tunes, light opera, till at the end of each evening, he would ask the audience to solemnly rise as he farted out *La Marseillaise*. "So great was his popularity, a shining beacon and logical end for all artists who aspire to an audience," Composer would conclude, "that he earned one hundred times more than the dozen top opera singers of the day combined."

"I've only come to see that there's another lesson in *Yankee Doodle*," Composer now answered somberly: "That a penny whistle can lighten the human heart." Looking up from his clasped hands he added, "And what's so wrong with that?"

In OZ, vanilla is called Crema de las Angelitas.

In IN, the main street is named Main Street.

CHAPTER TWENTY

Each dawn, Mechanic pushed his car up the steep slope of the bridge to the booth where he worked. $1.00...$1.00...$1.00.... Each sundown he struggled to hold back his car by its rear bumper so it wouldn't get away as he guided it back to its garage under the bridge. Each day he pushed it up, only to find himself the next day, like Sisyphus, pushing it up again. As he did, drivers whizzed by, shouting as they passed, "Get a horse!"

That vision he'd had of Poet (Sculptor) coasting downhill on her bike often came to him in those moments, her arms out in victory, hair whipping behind in the breeze, and the contrast made him wonder why both the going up and the coming down was so difficult for him.

In the evenings he worked on abandoned cars, unleashing his frustration and fantasies on their bodies.

In the morning, he would push his car uphill, other cars whizzing past, their horns blaring as he imagined he was leaving IN. Yet at day's end, he would return, the bumper of his car straining to escape his grip, his heels dug in to slow its descent as he was dragged behind by gravity and inertia.

Returned by nature to the garage he had set out from that morning, he would sit on its lift at the center of its concrete floor—an inmate of his own life, yet also its exile. Banished by whom? he wondered, operating the hydraulic controls of the lift to rise. By himself, he knew, by his former life as a mechanic which he no longer fit. By his lack of imagination. The lift locked in its upper-most position, the same height—and no more—that it reached every time. By his inability to escape into the life of an artist, like Composer or Photographer, he had to admit, but also through the fault of his parents for not escaping for him and giving him a different life: peasants before him whose generic stock seemed to infuse his very cells....

His hands had already grown to a size and thickness that allowed their calluses to fit the locations of worn spots on the tools he inherited. His fingerprints, yellow swirls on work-hardened pads, made his hands resemble his father's so much that he had to blink to clear his mind and make his hands become once again his own. If having hands that "were his own" even made any sense.

"We are literally star dust," Photographer had said, explaining how the surface of the earth was the accumulation of billions of years of cosmic dust that had fallen from space: cosmic dust, or dirt, that mingled with the dust of all of their fathers and mothers, too, nourishing the plants and animals we eat, becoming the stuff of our cells, which once they die, return to dust. "All ancient cultures express this singular truth in their creation myths," he had said, "the Hebrews punning Adam—first man—with *Ad-ahma,* or dirt/earth, the Latins punning Humans with *humus,* mud again. Did you know that ninety percent of household dust is comprised of dead skin cells?" he asked. "Think of it, everywhere we look, dirt is turning into men and women who are turning into dust. What story could be more surreal than this, if by 'sur' we mean 'Super' and not 'Un'?" When Mechanic said he did not know, Photographer continued to explain how Poet (Sculptor) grasped the dust-to-dust palindrome more profoundly than any of them: this was why she took up dirt as her language; not all things can be said in every language even if language always shapes what is said. What she had to say was best put in a vocabulary of loam, of soil, of mud, of dust, of humus, of earth, of ground, of adobe, of alluvium, of silt, of clay, of sand, of sediment...."

Considering Designer?... Did this mean he had more or less hope for her?

He looked at the grime that blackened the lifeline in his palm. In anger he flung the tools off of the bench. How he wished he could just go back to repairing cars again. He hammered his anvil. Had he known the curse that was about to enter through his eyes the

— ⓪ —

day he had worked on that trannie, he knew, picking up the very screwdriver he had used to unbutton it, he would have used the screwdriver to instead gouge himself blind. He looked down into the glinting star of its point, bringing it slowly toward his eye....

A low moan came from the night outside the garage.

A prowler? He picked up his father's hammer, and tripped out into the yard, stubbing his toe over that small mound of dirt that kept appearing before his door: a small, breast-shaped hump that he leveled each time he tripped over it but that kept reappearing like some stubborn weed: a persistent weed-seed below, no doubt, trying to push up into the light.

The wind had shifted. Whereas earlier it had smelled of sludge, telling him that it blew from the east where the oil dump was located, he could now smell the stench of sulfur from the steel mills that took up all of the useable shoreline of IN's land-locked lake. The sky in that direction throbbed with the deep, reddish-brown of meat that had gone bad, the glow coming from the pouring of an ingot, he knew. But the red sky had never before throbbed in rhythm with the sound of heavy breathing—coming from?—

When he shielded his eyes from the glare of the security light buzzing over his back door, he could see—the dogs. The dogs had come back. Instead of running off to live in OZ as he had imagined, they had come home to him. And one, the bitch, was lying in the cage panting—pregnant—her swollen belly rising and falling like the exhaust lid of a diesel engine throbbing heavily in idle.

— ⓪ —

CHAPTER TWENTY-ONE

Designer tingled as technicians wheeled the metal mockup of the grill she had designed into the wind tunnel. This time for sure, she thought, her mind reeling with discarded sketches, then blueprints, as she watched the technicians bolt the carless grill to a test stand. She moved to the observation window that ran along the wind tunnel's length. Scores of clay mockups filled the room around her: prototypes that were actually half grills, the model-makers saving time by making only the left side of each prototype, then placing it against a mirror so that she would have the illusion of seeing the whole. Looking into these mirrors reflecting mirrors, she caught sight of that monstrosity someone had sent her and that now rested beside the bay doors, waiting to go out with the trash: a huge mangle of welded fenders and other parts from cars she had once designed, now disfigured and multiplied nightmarish-ly in the labyrinth of mirrors. Someone had used a welding torch to sign it, *A Secret Admirer*, and the sight of it gave her a chill. If it was an admirer, and not a psy-cho, why hadn't he used his name? Why had he mailed her the butchered parts of her children the way a sick-o might mail the ears or nose of a kidnapped child back to the mother?...

The wind tunnel began to hum. As the wind rush-ing through its funnel-shaped walls picked up speed, the sound coming from the auto grill increased in pitch as though it were a chrome slide-whistle. Only a slide-whistle that gave up a haunting note: the first note from a new instrument, not unlike the quavering sound that can be elicited from the wet rim of a wine glass, only in the wind tunnel mechanically prolonged. Not the music of the spheres, nor that pathetic sound-less music, but something between the elevator music and the beauty of the silent music played by the night sky. An ethereal tone that seemed to come from some-where between the lowest sphere of heaven and the highest peak on earth.

Technicians, and model makers, and prototype fab-ricators and others that had helped to make the test a success let out a loud cheer. *"Bravo! Bravissimo!"* they shouted, turning to her to applaud.

"Yes!" she replied, fist in air. She had her instru-ment. Now all she needed was her Mallarmé to bring from it glorious musik.

CHAPTER TWENTY-TWO

As though on cue, just as Mechanic arrived at the address Photographer had given him there was a sudden *Crack!-thud* and his car became as immobile as a tree. Walking out from behind the trunk, he immediately saw the problem: one of the welds that held the door under the axle as a ski had broken. The car listed badly to the front-passenger side, where the break was located, and the sight of it wearied him. After finding the note Photographer had left, telling him when and where to meet, he had set out in plenty of time. But as he pushed his car, he had gotten lost in his thoughts over recent events, and had forgotten completely about their meeting until coming out of his mental wandering, he discovered that his pushing had brought him to the correct block anyway. Then this—

The jack was still in the trunk, he considered, sitting down on the curb. It had been left there from the days when the car used to go about on tires instead of skis. But his welding equipment was back at his garage, of course, and the dilemma seemed to express his life. As he ran through various options for bringing the broken car and his welding equipment together—tow the car there? bring the equipment here?—a darkening self-doubt began to seep over him. Would repairing the ski be no different than making any repair? That is, if putting a door in the place of a tire kept people from taking wheels for granted, would repairing the ski help him take skis for granted? If familiarity could make anything invisible, he thought, growing sicker by the minute, had a car with skis for wheels become invisible to him? Was he no better than those philistines, as Photographer called them, who insisted on cars with tires? Just in a different, i.e., worse, way?—a hypocrite?

Rising, he circled his sagging car, wondering what to do, the questions only leading him down a labyrinth of further questions. Would having his car towed be any different than driving a car with wheels himself?... He didn't know the neighborhood he was in, or even how far from home he had gone, but judging from the weariness of his muscles, the welder and the car were very far apart.

Photographer, he remembered, Photographer would know what to do and he was right here.

The building that the car had run aground before was plain even by IN standards, its windows boarded

$$- \text{\textcircled{0}} -$$

up in the manner of porno shops. Checking the address again, Mechanic confirmed that he was indeed in the right place. BOOKS said block lettering on the door.

Entering, Mechanic was surprised to see that the place was indeed a bookstore and not a bar. He didn't know there were any bookstores in IN, or that they only sold repair manuals. The metal shelves of manuals were arranged by genres of machines, from hair dryers and pencil sharpeners all the way up to entire industrial plants. Wandering the aisles, looking for Photographer, Mechanic paused here and there to thumb through the occasional title that caught his eye. Most of them seemed to be just light reading, exploded diagrams and instructions for making repairs to machines that were so simple, the repair of them seemed intuitive. He couldn't imagine anyone reading these books, let alone taking the time to write out the detailed instructions they contained. Others were for machines that performed functions so abstract he couldn't even imagine what need had brought them into existence, or the principles that made them operate, let alone who the books could have possibly been written for.

Looking up at their spines as he walked, he accidentally kicked into a folding chair—a line of metal folding chairs that had been set up in the aisle near the back of the store. At the head of the line of four or five chairs was a podium and standing at the podium was Poet (Sculptor).

— ◍ —

She went motionless when she saw that he saw her, glanced away, then back, then gave a little finger wave.

A rush of confusion went through him—the unexpectedness, the disorientation of suddenly coming upon her—but in the confusion was a sense of relief, coming upon a familiar face after the trials of the day. She did seem glad to see him. Still, unlike their encounter on the toll road and the comforting narrow bounds that the toll lane had put upon what he was supposed to say, making his way between the chairs and shelves of books on either side, the open-endedness of this situation filled him with terror. Should he just pretend he didn't recognize her? Turn and run?—no, he realized, remembering the sad way his broken car listed out in the street. He had to say something, but what? "Are you?—" he tried, nearing. "Are you buying a book?"

'No. Selling,' she said, by way of shaking her head, then pointing to the name tag pinned to her work shirt: SALES ASSOCIATE.

"You work here?"

She smiled, nodding sheepishly.

Encouraged to see that the narrow aisle between bookshelves was very much like the lane of a tollbooth, he determined to not sound like the mo-ped he had been the last time. "Then can you show me where you keep your manuals on— On? On hydraulic brakes?"

"Shhhhhhhhhhhhhhhhhhhhhhhhhhhhhhh!" someone hissed rudely. Turning around, Mechanic found Photographer sitting in one of the metal folding chairs he had just walked past. Photographer whispered loudly, "There'll be a book signing afterwards; you can ask questions then."

Book signing? Poet (Sculptor) was standing behind a podium, an open book on the podium, a microphone adjusted to her height, and the truth of what was happening dawned on Mechanic. She was giving a?— A reading?—a *poetry* reading?

"Oh, I'm sorry!" he exclaimed, stumbling to take a seat—where?—upfront? All three of the chairs in the line were empty and it was hard to decide. Agitated, Photographer motioned for him to sit in the one before him. "I didn't realize!..." Mechanic stuttered, stumbling into it.

She nodded that it was okay, that no harm had been done, then continued.

"Where have you been?" Photographer snapped, leaning forward to whisper sharply in Mechanic's ear. "Didn't you get my note?" As was his custom, he had tied it to a brick and then dropped the brick onto the roof of Mechanic's house so he would be alerted by the racket of the dogs it would set off. "You were supposed to have been here twenty minutes ago."

"I-I got lost," Mechanic whispered back. Poet (Sculptor) stood at the podium, turning pages, her eyes and finger moving down each page as she silently read. "Why didn't you tell me she was giving a reading?"

"She's not the type to brag," he answered cryptically. "But it's good you've come. I don't know where Composer is...."

Composer, Mechanic thought heavily.

"...it's the last book she created before she took up dirt as her medium. The publisher—a small experimental press—brought it out two years late," Photographer explained, "so it's important we support her. She was supposed to go on a book tour, but this was the only store that would have her. And they only did it because she works here."

Watching her silently read from her work, her lips moving, Mechanic began to understand how Photographer communicated so easily with her, how his own parents had found the need to speak lessen as their fifty-year marriage wore on until finally all they had to do to let the other know what they were thinking was to be in the same room. Somehow, sitting there before her, not expected to speak, under no pressure to carry his end, or both ends of a conversation, it was easier to listen. Or rather, an understanding of what she was saying would come over him though she spoke no words, the wrinkle of her forehead speaking volumes, as did the arch of an eyebrow, a frown, or twitch so subtle that he would never have even seen it before, looking down at his shoes as he struggled to come up with something to say.

Afterwards, the two men went up to congratulate her, and Mechanic thought that at least now he knew that she was a poet. But her book, *The Machine That Never Works: A Manual,* was thick as his fist, and shaped like a schematic symbol for—what? A valve? A heart? That is, it was a sculpture, and opening it he expected its inside to be blank: for if what she read

— ⓪ —

resulted in silence, what she read must have been blank. She wasn't mute. He had asked Photographer about that after meeting her and according to him she actually had a beautiful reading/singing voice. It's just that after taking up dirt as her medium, she wouldn't use it any longer. Unless there was something really worth saying. And her silence *did* point out how trite, how unnecessary most, if not all, conversation actually was. But this book *was* her work, after all, so if she didn't speak it, what else could she possibly consider worth saying?

But the book wasn't blank at all. When he opened it up, visual poems poured out: warranty cards, blueprints; a wiring-harness diagram folded out into a geodesic dome the size of a bread-box: a book of poetry that was a sculpture, or a sculpture in the form of a book that was poetry? Thumbing through its pages, trying to imagine what machine all the documents and drawings could refer to, he began to wonder if by "work" she meant "labor."

Photographer grabbed the book from his hands, then handed it to her for an autograph.

"I would like to buy a copy also," Mechanic said, drawing out his wallet, miffed by the way Photographer had snatched the book away.

Poet (Sculptor) pretended as if she hadn't heard him, her tongue stuck out in concentration as she fashioned a dedication to Photographer in the book's flyleaf—more of a drawing than a signature.

"Are you sure?" Photographer asked. "Each book is twenty-five thousand dollars, you know."

— ⓪ —

"Twenty-five thousand dollars?" Mechanic repeated, looking at the two limp bills in his billfold.

"And it's sold. As in 'Sold out.' The entire print run has sold out."

"Your book has sold out?" Mechanic repeated, incredulous. And not a little relieved. "That's fantastic!"

Poet (Sculptor) shrugged.

"Of course there was only one copy," Photographer said, making Mechanic afraid that he had accidentally slighted her again, that she had shrugged out of embarrassment for having such a small print run. "Mine."

Or was she embarrassed for him, shrugging to minimize her victory because she was a good sport, a good winner, having sold every copy while she knew the difficulty he was having in getting an audience for his work. She looked back down into the elaborate signature/dedication she was drawing for Photographer.

"When the philistine publisher who held her manuscript hostage learned how much the book would cost to produce," Photographer was explaining, "they tried to back out. They claimed that the special dies and plates that were needed to make her manuscript into the three-dimensional book she wanted would bankrupt their little kitchen-table operation. But she had a contract, and if she eliminated the sculptural nature that made her book her book it wouldn't be her book. It would be nothing, so what would be the point? It was difficult, very difficult, huh?" he asked Poet (Sculptor). Her smile twist into a wry look as though remembering a war story, or a story of a mass migration that had turned out well, though it was nonetheless still painful. "Many times she nearly gave in but I wouldn't let her eliminate a single Braille dot," he said, winking happily at Poet (Sculptor). "Unfortunately, its production costs did consume all of the publisher's assets, and in the end, the strain to bring out this one copy cost them their office, that is their kitchen, along with the rest of the business, that is their house.

"But the true bottom line is that the book came into the world in the form it was meant to be, I was able to buy it, and since the publishers put such a high price on the book, they will be sure to reopen their doors. Or at least open a new kitchen-table operation under a different name. So you see, it was a win-win situation!"

Mechanic said nothing, remembering how his own mechanic's business had gone under. Would he have been better off compromising? What would that even mean? Making every other repair regular? Repairing every car half way?... He sighed heavily, wishing he had looked harder for a way to stay out of the tollbooth....

"Don't look so disappointed," Photographer said, turning the book to look when she had finished the dedication, "now that the book has sold out, there's sure to be a second printing. We are in negotiations with the publisher right now. Or at least will be once they return my calls, isn't that right?" Photographer didn't allow her to release the book as he took it from her, though. Instead, he took Mechanic's hand and placed it on top of hers. "Now that the publishers real-ize what they should have thought of before they even went into publishing," he said, bobbing the book in

— ⓪ —

cadence with their hands upon it. "Your art, your life, your love is not the place to be timid." He pronounced the words solemnly, looking directly at her as though he was some kind of judge, or minister conducting a ceremony with the book between them, and the emotionless mask that her face became, the way her eyes refused to meet Mechanic's was as meaningful as some secret handshake he had been allowed to participate in, if not understand.

CHAPTER TWENTY-THREE

"When I took my job at the tollbooth," Mechanic lamented to Photographer, back in Photographer's camera-house after the reading, after the two of them had labored for the rest of the day to get his broken car back to Mechanic's garage, " I thought I would enjoy swimming in a sea of cars." The oceanic hiss and rush of cars on the bridge continued its accompaniment beneath their feet. "But I didn't figure on how depressing the drivers could be, only concerned with getting from point A to point B, never giving their vehicles a thought unless it was to gild these lilies by the addition of fuzzy dice, or toy dogs whose heads bob up and down."

"Tsk, tsk," Photographer sighed sympathetically. "Perhaps you would be happier in a less people-oriented line of work, like gravedigger." He poured Mechanic another cup of tea.

"Sometimes I feel like such a fool." He pointed to his name stitched over his shirt pocket. "The toll-road uniform is exactly the same as my old mechanic's uniform. I didn't even have to change clothes."

"Ach, don't be so hard on yourself," Photographer scoffed, hearing none of it. "What else were you to do?—Go on making '*repairs*'? Only a werewolf can write like a court reporter all day and howl poems at the moon by night. That's why I quit making photographs with film entirely."

"But even if I take off this uniform," Mechanic said, trying to make his point clearer, "under my clothes my body is still the same."

Photographer pulled his chair closer. "Listen my friend, let me tell you a story. At my darkest moment, when all the world told me that I was crazy for wanting to change the world with my movies—*Ha!*—I began—like you—to wonder if in fact black was white and white, like they said, black. But chance, or Zeus, or fate or whatever it is that sends to us what we most need in our hour of need, sent to me a story from my youth, the story of Adam's Peak: the highest point on earth, protruding from The Garden of Eden to a height half way between the strife of the earth's surface and the serenity of the lowest sphere of heaven, the moon. From this peak, it was said, Adam could hold the entire world in one, unframed view—and I clung to this story as if my life depended on it. This is why I moved to this house atop the toll bridge. At the time, it was the highest point around, even higher than OZ. A person could see all the way to the sea from this spot. But then, of course, OZ grew like a new mountain range, blocking the view. No matter, that was also about the time I realized I was losing my sight."

"What do you mean you're losing your sight?" Mechanic asked, recalling a creeping stiffness in his own fingers that made it increasingly difficult to hold a wrench.

Photographer nodded. " I am going blind."

"No!"

"All those years of standing in the place of film, focusing light on my eyes, is making them useless. So I practice by closing my eyes. And I discovered that if the essence of photography is seeing, the essence of seeing is the mind."

"You mean you are actually losing your sight?"

"From that day on, I determined to make a genre of photography no one else could see, one that when I died, would die with me—and that, my friend, is the essence of art. And of life." He paused a moment, then added, "And that is also why she has feelings for you."

"She?" A wild hope went through Mechanic, thinking for a minute that Photographer had meant Designer. But seeing him nod solemnly, it became clear why Photographer had insisted he attend the meeting of the Anti-Billboardistas; why he had called him a blockhead that night after the concert; why he had been agitated at Mechanic for nearly missing a reading. All of these instances had one common denominator. "She told you that?" he asked.

"Not in words, of course." He pulled something out from under his chair. A bicycle chain. One of its

— ⊙ —

links was missing. And Mechanic came to know that it was from her bicycle and that she wanted him to fix it.

Only a few short months ago, he would have known what to do with a clarity that he had never had before or since. A friend who would ask him to make a repair could be no friend. Could be only an enemy, a brute without the slightest understanding of him or his work. And Photographer would have agreed. But now, looking at the rusted chain draped between Photographer's two fists, its stiff links bowed into the outline of a valentine, Mechanic was so confused he wanted to cry.

So Photographer couldn't see the emotion coming over him, he pushed his face in his hands.

"Let me explain with another story," Photographer said. "For different stories are meaningful to us at different times in our lives. Isn't that right? The Sur myth for an artist is not the story of Adam's Peak, I, now wiser, understand, but The Tower of Babel, though the tower gets far too much attention in most re-tellings of the story. For you see, God's wrath wasn't over the tower, the presumption of man making an artificial Adam's peak out of brick. As it says in the Bible, the people of Babel only set out on this project because they wanted to make a name for themselves. In other words, take possession of language, what made humans human. And God, being the ironic comedian that He is, always gets even with His challengers by giving them what they want. In spades. 'You want language, then here's language!' He thundered, His Voice so powerful

— ⓪ —

that its sound shattered the one tongue they spoke into many—making them even more human.

"Yet, therein lies the first of two lessons any artist can live by: to resolve yourself to an earnestness of such intensity that you will succeed gloriously—or fail so tragically that your failure will become as legendary as success—the inevitable fate of a mortal who challenges the gods. For you see, though God knocked down their tower, scattered their tongue, the people of Babel did make a name for themselves, as we prove each time we re-tell the story of their failure. And that name is 'people,' i.e., all of us."

"And the other lesson?" Mechanic asked.

"Live where you work," Photographer said, tapping his skull. He closed his eyes. "Work where you live," he added, tapping his skull as he continued, "Pracuj tam, kde žiješ," and "Vive donde trabajas," and "Leofa flær flu wyrcst," and "Да живееш където работиш,"and "Tinggallah dimana saudara bekerja," and "Vivez où vous travaillez," and "Ni zhai na ni gong zuo jiu zhai na ni sheng huo," and "Hataraku tokoro wa seikatsu no ba de aru," and "Vive ubi laboras," and "Mieszkaj gdzie pracujesz," and "Woon waar je werkt," and " कर्मक्षेत्र ईवा वासेत ,"and "Vivi dove lavori," and "Woon waar jy werk," and " Живіть там, де працюєте ," and "Lebe wo du arbeitest," and "Auskon aeina tashtaghel," and " 生活中工作，工作中生活 ," and "Viva onde trabalha," and "Bo hvor du arbeider," and "Goor aeifo ta'vod." He opened his mouth to an 'O' and popped it with the flat of his hand to sound ".-.. ..

...-. / .-- .... . .-. / -.-- --- .. / .-- --- .-. -.- .-.-.- ." He continued tapping his skull, saying, "Menya okhola mirimo," and " 행위가 있는 곳에 존재가 있고 ," and "Dzīvo tur, kur tu strādā," and "Zhivi, gde rabotaesh'," and "Yoo tee tum ngahn," and " 在 你 工作 之 地 安 居 ," and "Hidup dimana kamu bekerja," and "Hidup lah dimana anda bertugas," and " 働く 所に 住め ," and "Bo hvor du arbeider." Turning his hands into a language, he signed: " 🤟 ✊ 👌 🤝 ." Then he said, " Δουλέυετε ὅπου ζεῖτε," and "Elä, missä työskentelet," and "Bo där du arbetar," and " ᐊᑯᑉ ᖃᐅ ᖅᐅ ᐃᐅᖁᖅ ," and " जहाँ निवास करो वहाँ काम करो," and "Živi tamo gdje radiš," and "Gyvenk ten, kur dirbi," and "Manum operi qua vixi," and " གནས་ས་དེ་ལ་ལས། ," and "Strādājiet tur, kur dzīvojiet!" and "Där jaii ke kar mikåni zendegi kån," and "

在
你
工
作
之
地
安
居
,

." He scratched out on his floor:

🐂𓏤🦅𓃭𓆓𓅱𓃭𓏏𓅱𓅱𓏤⌒.

Then: " ᚦᛦᚼᚠ ᚱᛅ ᚱᛅᚠ ᚤᛅ ᚱᛅᛦ ."
Then: " Ապրիր որտեղ աշխատում ես ." Then he led Mechanic's hands over rocks he had arranged as:

⠚⠊⠧⠑⠀⠺⠓⠑⠗⠑⠀⠽⠕⠥⠀⠺⠕⠗⠅⠲

"Ishi unapofanya kazi," he said, and "Elage, kus töö-
tate," and "Sống tại nơi bạn làm việc," and "Žij tam, kde
pracuješ," and "**Locuiţi unde lucraţi**," and "Živi le tam,
kjer delaë," and "Tix-oi dewk-a skan se-veh," and
"Log i kien al ci funkcii," and "જ્યા કામ કરો છો ત્યાના થઈ જાવ,"
and "Tinggallah dimana saudara bekerja," and "Ott
lakj, ahol dolgozol," and "زندگی جاي کن که کار ميکنی," and
"Woon waar je werkt," and "**çalıştığın yerde yaşa**,"
and "تجاي که کار ميکنی بسر بير" and "Jeto aty ku punon,"
and "Tshela ko o berekang keng," and "وہاں و رہائش
جہاں و کام," and "Zivi tamo gde radiš...."

He sucked in breath so deep it seemed to turn him
inside out, making of his body a mirror of breath giving back the identical idea, only different: "Radi tamo
gde zivis," and "رہائش و وہاں، کام و جہاں," and "Bereka
ko o tshelang teng," and "Puno aty ku jeton," and
"جاي که بسر می بری کار کن," and "Yasadigin yerde çalis,"
and "**yaşadiğin yerde çalış**," and "کار در جاي کن زندگی ميکنی,"
and "Werk waar je woont," and "Strādā tur, kur tu
dzīvo," and "Ott dolgozz, ahol laksz," and "Bekerjalah
dimana saudara tinggal," and "**Lucraţi unde locuiţi**," and
"જ્યા રહો છો ત્યાંજ કામ કરો," and "Delaj le tam, kjer živiš," and
"Làm việc tại nơi bạn sống," and "Pracuj tam, kde žiješ,"
and "Vivo qua opus," and "Na ufanye kazi unapoishi,"
and "جاي که بسر می بری کار کن" Again he made his hands
speak their silent language: "🤙 🤟 👊 🖐." Again he
made rocks speak: ⠩⠲⠺⠉ ⠹⠺⠈⠉⠺ ⠺⠺⠂⠺
⠹ ⠺⠹⠂ ⠈⠺⠂. Again with the "Да работиш където
живееш," and the "Աշխատիր որտեղ ապրում ես."
Again with the scratching: 𓂀𓂀 ▬ ▬ 𓂀𓅐 ▬ 𓅐 𓏥𓂸
𓊪𓌳 𓅐. "Labora ubi vivis," he said, and "Dzīvojiet

tur, kur strādājiet! " Still tapping his skull he said, "Töötage, kus elate!" and " ཝས་ས་དེ་ལ་གནས། ," and "Dirbk ten, kur gyveni," and " कर्म त्यहाँ जहाँ जीवन छ ," and "Radi tamo gdje zivis," and "Arbeta där du bor," and " Ζεῖτε ὅπου δουλέυετε ," and "Ttyöskentele, missä elät," and "Arbejd hvor du bor," and " कर्म भूमि में निवास करो," and "Pracujesz gdzie żyjesz," and " ౬౦౦౦ ౧౦ ౦౦ ౬౦౦, " and "Bekerjalah dimana anda hidup," and "Tum ngahn tee yoo," and "

在
你
乐
居
之
地
工
作

," and "Na ukhole mirimo awamenya," and " ໄຕ໖ ໂ∏ ໂໃ ⍲໖). " Again with the popping of the mouth: ".-- --- .-. -.- / .-- .... . -.. / -.-- --- ..- / .-.. .. ...- . .-.-.- ." Then "Rabotai, gde zhivesh'," and "Ta'vod aeifo ata gar," and "Arbeide hvor du bor," and " ⌐⁊⁊ᒿ ⌐⁊ ⌐⁊ᒿ⌐ ⍾⁊⟋ ⌐⁊⊣⌐⟋, " "Trabalhe onde vive," and "Se-veh dewk-a skan tix-oi," and "Funkcii kien al ci log i," and "Eshtaghel aeina taskon," and " 在 你 乐 居 之 地 工 作, " and "Arbeite wo du lebst," and " निवासस्थाने अपि कार्यम कुर्यात , " and "Lavori dove vivi," and "Werk waar jy woon," and "Där jaii ke zendegi mikåni kar kån," and "Werk waar je woont," and "Prqcuj gdzic mieskasz," and "Seikatsu wa hataraku ba de aru," and "Travailles où tu vis," and

"Ni zhai na ni sheng huo, ni jiu zhai na ni gong zuo," and "Trabaja donde vives," and "Ži tam, kde pracuješ," and "Wyrce flær flu leofast...."

When Photographer had finished working his way through some six thousand living languages, and many dead, Mechanic asked, "Would you tell this to Composer?"

CHAPTER TWENTY-FOUR

"Wyrce flær flu leofast," Photographer told Composer, finishing his story this time the way others used to say "Remember the Alamo."

He and Mechanic looked to Composer for his reaction. Composer paced about The Essence of IN Hole, hands clasped white-knuckled behind his back, his brow furrowed. High above, the mouth of the hole framed the night sky like the viewfinder of a box camera. Since this hole was far enough from town and deep enough to block out all artificial light, it was the only dwelling in either OZ or IN from which the stars were visible.

Composer began speaking softly, as though making a confession. "Everyone has heard of The Tower of Babel," he said. "Less well known is The Tunnel of Babel. As you say, the tower wasn't the issue at all. It wasn't even what the people necessarily wanted to build. True enough, what they really wanted to make was a name for themselves. Building a tower that could reach to god seemed about as good a way as any to do so. Though god wanted to keep them at arms' length, they were his children, and being children of god, they too had a sense of irony. After god knocked down their tower, the people of Babel began to dig. If god wouldn't let them create a Sur myth, they reasoned, they would create an Ur myth. For, quite naturally, they thought language was already theirs. Hadn't god left it up to them to invent, indeed, had not god made it a part of the human condition by allowing Adam to create it as he did, crying out every mineral, vegetable, and animal's name, his every utterance the birth of a new word? With only one person giving names, every word matched exactly one thing, as a tree casts a shadow. When Adam said, cat, he didn't confuse it with a jazz musician. Language was like a rock or a tree—a natural object— until god scattered their tongue. So being ironic comedians themselves, they said, 'If you want to knock down our creation, all right, go ahead. But you cannot do it without our help,' and they began to dig. They dug a tunnel that undermined the foundation of not only their own tower but of all buildings. Those edifices that were the heaviest, the institutions, leaned cockeyed, then fell with the loudest crashes. It was the deconstruction of Babel, if you will, and by digging it they made themselves a name—'people,' that is, no one in particular. And that is the lesson we live with to this day. Which is to say, I just can't say what is right any more."

— ⓪ —

CHAPTER TWENTY-FIVE

$1.00...$1.00...$1.00...$1.00... A white sedan with the humped shape of wings or fins slowed as it approached his booth, and mechanically, Mechanic stuck out his hand. The driver—HER—fished pennies from the built-in coin holder on her dash, then dropped them into his hand, saying "Thank you" to his hand, never looking up to his face, then driving on and he stood there staring at his hand, a strong wind blowing the pennies out of it as if they were leafs in a pile before an approaching gale.

For the rest of the day he kept watching the traffic in the other direction, waiting to see if Designer returned to OZ. She never came. That evening, he dug his heels into the pavement as he was pulled home, staring the whole while at his hands gripping the bumper, trying to hold back the momentum of the car yearning for the bottom. The gears of his mind ground with the memory of his hand, too stiff to close around the pile of pennies Designer had placed in it before the wind flicked them away one at a time till there was nothing left, only an empty palm that had the exact size, shape and lifelines as his father's hand.

When he stubbed his toe on the mound of dirt that had reappeared before his door, he stomped it flat, and stomped it flat, and stomped, and kept stomping till he wore himself out with stomping. Live where you work, he kept hearing in his mind—while SHE was spending the night in HIS hole. He knew she was because he could hear the sound of distant singing, and he didn't need to go there to know where it was coming from. He sat in his garage, hands clamped over his ears, fighting to ignore the sound, the low singing growing through the course of the evening until it became a yowl, and he couldn't stand it anymore.

Outside, he found one of his dogs howling in pain—a pup was coming out of her. But something had gone wrong and it was stuck. The male dog raced around in a circle, yapping madly. "Work where you live," Mechanic told her, stroking her fur and getting down on a knee to have a look. He stuck a finger in the slimy suck of the bitch's bottom. Had the dogs ever left him? he wondered. Three other pups, all covered with afterbirth, were already lying on the ground mewing. He used to lie in bed imagining his dogs running all the way to OZ and romping through its luxurious

— 0 —

trash. But now he doubted they had ever really left. He helped the next pup out, its mucousy body suddenly in his hands, afterbirth dripping like snot from his fingers. This pup looked exactly like the other ones, exactly like the mother, and the father. Using both hands, he helped birth two more pups, hoping they might explain the world to him. Each one was dark-haired, with identical pointed ears. Not one bird. Not one cat. He went back into the garage.

The furnace roared, the mill-stone of the forge's counterweight slowly ground in its orbit mesmerizing him the way a person standing at the edge of a great height feels the seduction of surrender. Mechanic slowly brought his fingertips near. His right arm, the arm he extended and retracted from his booth a thousand times a day had begun to take on the angular dimensions of an endurance runner, while his left arm, and his middle, and his hands had begun to go soft. What had been most essential about his work, he saw, was his han—

With a scream he realized his hand was under the crushing kiss of the counterweight.

CHAPTER TWENTY-SIX

Photographer was standing in his camera, sunlight streaming in on his closed eyes when he heard it: a whistling so ethereal that at first he thought it was the song angels sing when a soul departs the earth. He raced to the window-aperture of his house to look out at the cars below, the whistling growing louder. Though his eyes were too clouded to see so far, he didn't need them to tell that the music was coming from a white car. Then, there it was, slowing to pay its toll. It went out of sight again as it glided beneath his home and fell silent. A moment later it started up again, and he raced to the opposite window to watch, the ethereal whistling singing an accompaniment to the prayer for the dead he recited, the car receding as it continued on its way to OZ.

— ⓪ —

CHAPTER TWENTY-SEVEN

Mechanic also heard the ethereal singing. He had been lying in bed, wondering if the reason he could never remember whether Photographer's friend was a Poet or a Sculptor was because to her there was no difference. And since there was no difference, there was no word. Then he heard the whistling. To him it sounded like the song mermaids sing deep in the sea as they glide about their work of rescuing drowning sailors. The dull ache of his bandaged hand seemed to throb in rhythm, the way the rushing of the sea that a person hears when they put a conch shell to their ear was actually the roar of their own blood reverberating in the shell, and therefore in the mind. When he stilled his hand to listen, the singing stopped. Just when he thought it had only been in his mind, though, he heard it again, high above, it seemed, but fading this time, and he remained very still so he could hear it as long as possible, straining now to believe that the singing was coming from within but afraid it was simply continuing on without him....

A clatter out in the yard startled him.

Opening the door he found Poet (Sculptor) on a knee before a small mound of dirt—the tiny mound he had tripped over, then stomped flat. It was her mound, he now saw, and she was restoring it. Beyond her, out in the yard, her bicycle had fallen against the garage. The dogs were calmly sniffing its seat. The small sprocket that made the rear wheel turn was a golden rust-brown in the sunlight. The large sprocket that the pedals turned was right out in the open too, exposed as it was without a chain guard. And he was moved by the beauty of the machine's simple logic, the teeth of its gears visible as they were, chainless as they were, the chain she had wanted him to fix still hanging like a limp line from a nail inside the garage.

He raised a hand to point to the garage, to tell her he had her chain and hadn't forgotten about it. But as he did, she rose, catching sight of his bandaged hand, and she gasped, taking it in her own dirty fingers, and saying, "You're hurt."